THE PRIVATE LETTERS OF LUKE

ROGER LLOYD

The Private Letters
of Luke

CHANNEL PRESS

GREAT NECK, NEW YORK

Printed in the United States of America

Library of Congress Catalog Card Number, 57-12035

CONTENTS

PART ONE

PART TWO

PREFACE

It is not the function of a preface to make excuses or to forestall criticism, and ordinarily a book ought to stand on its own feet, and to explain itself. But when a book is an imaginary reconstruction of the life of so universally beloved and familiar a saint as Luke the Physician, a certain amount of preliminary explanation both of the characters and of the episodes invented for them does become necessary. This book is certainly a work of fiction, not of history or of biblical criticism. But all the characters, except for one, appear if only as names, and most of them as far more than names, in the New Testament, and all the episodes are related to known facts, or are at least reasonable inferences from them. Something, therefore, does need to be said about the relationship of conjecture to fact in the invented correspondence which follows.

Any book about St. Luke which strays beyond the field of a commentary on his writings is bound to be a work of fiction. The certain historical facts we know about him are few indeed. He was a doctor. He was much loved. He was the friend and travelling companion of St. Paul, and the friend of his friends. He wrote the third gospel and the book of the Acts of the Apostles, and from the passages in the latter where he writes We instead of They, we can trace some of his movements. But that is all and the rest is conjecture. But while conjecture must always be labelled as such and not concealed, it need not be wild or improbable as long as it is kept in line with logically and psychologically reasonable inferences from the known facts. For example, it is a tradition and not a proved fact that Luke lived for some years in Antioch and there became a member of the Christian local congregation. But this is so overwhelmingly probable, and makes sense of other facts

which if it were not true would remain disconnected, that to
refuse to accept it because it cannot now be exactly proved
is to carry scholarly and legal caution to lengths inappro-
priate in a work of fiction.

There are, however, two other facts about St. Luke which
are as certain as anything in this dubious world can be. The
first set of facts concerns the kind of man he was and his
attitude to life. He was a very good and deeply compassionate
doctor whose practice had bred in him a deep understanding
of women and a profound, even an indignant sympathy with
the hopeless sufferings of the poor. He had a deep hostility to
the power of wealth, which is not at all the same thing as
saying that he disliked and distrusted all rich people just
because they were rich. But he had his austere side. Once a
man had become a Christian he was rightly to be judged, in
St. Luke's view, by far severer standards than would have
been appropriate to apply to him while still a heathen. It is
certain, too, that though he was the steadiest of all St. Paul's
friends, his profound admirer, and his constant companion,
he did not see in Christianity exactly the same values in the
same order of importance that St. Paul saw. In his writings he
neither endorses nor criticises what is called the Pauline
Gospel. He simply ignores it, though he had heard his friend
utter it a thousand times. That is fact, and Letter XXIV tries
to explain the fact. In this it is like practically all the other
letters, which are really fictitious embroideries or variations
on factual themes.

The other undeniable fact about St. Luke is the appeal he
has always made to Christian imagination, and never more
strongly than today. Among all the characters in the New
Testament it is he that we should most like to meet, and with
him we think we should be most at home and at ease. The
fact that we know little about him for certain does not shake
our conviction that if we knew all we should not be less

attracted by the whole than we are by the part. My own attraction is lifelong, and of all the people in history I suppose I think most often about two, Shakespeare and St. Luke. You cannot constantly think about St. Luke without forming your own convictions, and creating your own vivid pictures of the sort of man he was, what he looked like, how he became a Christian, and why he accepted the vocation to write the stories of Jesus' life and the adventures of the Apostles. The guesses you make about these things, and the bridges you imaginatively build to carry you over the gaps in the narrative gradually become convictions. As long as they make a psychologically consistent picture, though unprovable, they may well be true. This, at any rate, is the St. Luke of my imagination; and I do not believe he is wildly different from the first century Greek physician–evangelist whom St. Paul and Silvanus and so many other New Testament characters knew well and loved dearly.

He was not a solitary and not a quietist. More perhaps than most saints he can be seen only as a figure in a crowded scene, quick with action. Any account of him must therefore be an account of at least some of the other Christians he knew. I have therefore written this book in the form of a series of letters by him, to him, and about him. All his correspondents except for Issachar occur in the New Testament. Of some of them, Silvanus and Barnabas, we know as much or more than we do of St. Luke. Theophilus is almost pure guesswork. To him he dedicated both his books: 'It seemed good to me to write unto thee, most excellent Theophilus, that thou mightest know the certainty of those things wherein thou has been instructed'. The salutation, 'Your Excellency', gives him high official position; 'that he had been instructed', makes it clear that he had become a Christian. Any further identification is a matter of guesswork alone, and an author is free to make a Theophilus to serve his own purpose. It

was artistically convenient that Luke should at some time
have cured the Roman Minister of State of his asthma, and
these statements have no other authority. Nor can I guarantee
that either Nicholas the Deacon or Persis the Public Scribe
were in life as I have imagined them in fiction. But I hope so.
Every church has need of simple and unpretentious heroes
and is saved in the end by its homespun saints. The scoundrelly
but tortured Issachar is pure invention, but St. Paul's letters
make it plain that there were plenty of Jews, and baptised
Christians among them, of the type and lineage of Issachar,
who did their not inconsiderable best to torment his life and
ruin his ministry.

Of the various episodes only three need a little explanation
here. That St. Luke suddenly appears in Troas is certain because
the 'We' passages in ACTS start at that point, and the imagined
riot in church in Antioch in Letter XVI provides a reason for
his going there. Letter XIX which brings Paul and his friends
to Luke at Troas when they had intended to be miles away
in Bythinia, and identifies Luke with the mysterious man of
Macedonia who cried 'Come over and help us', is an attempt
to wrench an intelligible story out of ACTS XVI, 6 to 12,
which is perhaps the most mysterious and difficult passage
anywhere in the Bible. That later St. Luke had two years to
spare, so to speak, while St. Paul was in protective custody in
Caesarea is certain fact. That he used it to travel about Palestine finding out all he could about the life of Christ is a conjecture of the overwhelmingly probable sort. It is certain that
he recorded many things in that Life which, as it seems, the
other evangelists did not know, and hardly less certain that
he discovered them by personal enquiry. If so, those two
years were the obvious time for the enquiry to be undertaken,
and probably the only time.

Among the facts which Luke alone seems to have known is
almost the whole of the Christmas story. All the scholars

whose learning gives them the right to judge agree that the first two chapters in his gospel—I, 5 to II, 40—came to him in the form of a Judean manuscript written in either Hebrew or Aramaic, that the literary style of this manuscript was rough and homespun, and that Luke simply transliterated it, word by word and phrase by phrase, from its original tongue to Greek, and that therefore the Greek of those two chapters is far from being the polished classical Greek which Luke instinctively used everywhere else. That much is as certain as anything well can be. But as to the manner in which Luke came by this priceless document not a single word is known, and therefore fancy is free to roam as it will, even to inventing a Bethlehem innkeeper as the intermediary. St. Paul's martyrdom is fictitious, but not in the sense that it may never have happened, but only in the sense that we do not know how or when. There are reasons for thinking that the Empress Poppaea's Jewish relations had something to do with it, and he of whom St. Paul wrote at the last, 'Only Luke is with me', would surely not be far from his master and his friend in the last ordeal.

ROGER LLOYD
Winchester
St. Luke's Day, 1956

PART ONE

FROM you, most even tempered of men and dearest of friends, I had not expected it. So frank a letter and so full and intimate an account of the depths of your mind is certainly a pledge of friendship, and naturally precious to me. To display gradually, layer by layer, the full range of their thoughts and moods is how friends ought to deal with each other; and when a man needs comfort, as you say you do, it is to his friend that he ought to turn. In so turning, he honours him, as you now honour me, and so I greatly rejoice in the trust you place in me. Yet I also grieve, and, more than this, am deeply puzzled by the sadness and disillusion which you say has overtaken you.

No, it is not the disease but the patient which baffles me. To live in Rome is to see the disease every day. It is perhaps the modern sickness of imperial society, so many there are out of whose lives all zest for living has fled. This is serious, because a mild infection in Rome, the heart of the world, soon becomes a raging epidemic in a score of provinces. But I did not know that the disease which caused old Fortunatus while still quite young to retire from the Senate and go to his farm in Umbria to spend the rest of his life growing roses, and drove Ventimilius to open his veins in his bath, had reached the very ends of empire in Syria. I could write you a long analysis of the causes of this disease, and diagnose its symptoms and effects. But not now—and anyway it is you who are the physician, while I am just the Emperor's servant who is bidden to remind him sometimes that he has an empire and to tell him a little about it, and about those who govern it. No, this frustration of modern life, as I often call it, is for you to describe to me, not me to you.

But I would not have thought that you, of all men, could ever have described it from your own personal experience. By their trade physicians ought to be immune, and among physicians, you most of all whom I know. Your life is creative. Your learning, your deep knowledge of all kinds of people, the trust they place in you, your ability to help them when sick, to ease their pain, to heal them, or, if it must be so, to make them ready to die in peace—all these things which are yours add up to the most complete of all lives, filled by an interest and satisfaction which it need never lose. A slave will and an imperial official may think his life hardly worth living. But not, surely, a doctor! Or if, here and there, you could find even a bored doctor, surely he would never be my best of friends and my most skilled of physicians.

Remember that I owe to you my life: The Emperor says that it is worth something to him, and it should be to you as you saved it for me, for him, and I hope for yourself as well. Had I not come to you in my need that day in Athens three years ago, I should certainly have been dead long since. But I came in despair and you gave me hope. I came in weakness and you gave me strength. I came in great sickness and you gave me health—and this health has stayed with me all the days since then.

Do I need to remind you who will certainly remember? For years I had been a victim of that disease of breath and lungs. It gripped me one night in the dark, and then it would play with me like a cat with a mouse. Without any warning that frightening, horrible sensation of choking would seize me. For a time the lungs seemed to be bursting, and the heart raced faster and faster. Each breath felt as though it must be the last breath. Stark black fear possessed me. I was utterly helpless, poised on the very rim of death. No physical sensation could be more terrifying. When at last the violence of the attack waned, and the exquisite relief of it followed, it left the victim spent and exhausted, and often took its departure with a final kick in the shape of some excruciating pangs of cramp, as though to say, 'That's all for now—but only for now'. There was never any knowing when the next attack would come. It might be tomorrow, or next week, or perhaps not for six months. But sooner or later come it would, and the whole of life was ruled by the fear of it. Those three years were horrible. Many a night I cried myself to sleep. No physician seemed able to help, and I tried many. I got to know so well the look on all their faces— compassionate but helpless. I know exactly what passed in poor Ventimilius' mind when he stumbled desperately to his bathroom, locked his door, lay down in his steaming bath, and then cut his main artery. More than once, you see, I got to the bathroom door myself, but always I fled in time. But the day would have come quite soon when desperation and hopelessness would have given me the courage (or the final cowardice —which is it?) to lock that door as Ventimilius did, and to reach for the razor.

But then, when I was near the last minutes of possible endurance, I came to you of whose praise I had heard in Athens, and on your face there was compassion but not helplessness. You said you could save me. You made me believe you could save me. You did save me. Since then the demon which governed my breathing has left me alone, and I know he will not come back. How you did it, what you had to give that others of your calling had not, I did not know then and have not known since. All I know is that through you, your faithfulness and skill, I had my life made new again, and at last worth the living.

Now I do not flatter myself that I am your only successful patient. What you have done for me, you must also have done for others. How can it be possible for any life spent in giving back life to seem weary and unprofitable? Of all the many men I know, I should say that none had more reason to go on his course rejoicing and with zest. You have made me anxious, my friend. Do write soon to tell me that your sadness, your gentle melancholy if you prefer that phrase, is a temporary illusion which has passed and changed. Nothing would give me more joy than to know you had once more found your joy, as I once received my life at your hands.

Luke to Theophilus

YOUR letter makes me ashamed of my outburst. The truth is that I never was and could never be a Stoic. I am not brave enough, and I do not believe in the stoic code. Suffering is like joy, meant to be shared. Though I spend my life fighting it I still believe that suffering has a purpose. It exists to create compassion. The more it is hidden the less compassion it creates. To wear the stoic mask of marble indifference over one's own suffering is to deny to it all possible relief, while that inhuman façade of detachment which the philosophers in the Schools so constantly advise physicians to put on means that no one will open their grief to us. It may save us from our own heartbreak, but unless we physicians are ready to let our hearts be broken sufferers must bear their pain in silence. Pain of body or mind must come out and be shared or there is no healing. That is the first principle of the physician's art, and if he is any good his heart is broken every day.

This seemingly vague but actually agonising depression of which I wrote may be unmanly, and if it is I must struggle against it and try to conquer it and put it away. It may be part of the whole sickness of imperial society, as you hint, and if it is I ought to grapple with it in myself, as it is my pledged life's work to fight sickness, not to succumb to it. That is why I began this letter to you by writing that I am ashamed of my outburst. But everything you have written to me suggests that you think I ought to find my clue through my profession, whereas the truth is that it is my profession which all the time implants the seeds of this disease—if disease it is—in me. You see, my dear friend, you know the physician's life so much less well than the imperial servant's life that really you do not know it at all. Forgive me, then, if I explain, even though this must mean that I open my grief still further before you.

The physician's calling is to fight disease. For that he is trained and for that he lives. But in spite of his training, which nowadays is elaborate and exact, there are still many diseases which he fights in vain. The weapons we have to fight disease are still very limited. In fact they really amount to only two. The first is a full knowledge of herbs and roots. We are all taught about them, where to find them and how to use them. You have to be a botanist before you can become a physician. Use the right herbs in the right way, and you can generally cure fevers of all kinds, ease the pain of sprains, and do much to put digestive disorders right. In fact herbs and roots are the basis of modern medicine, and with them a physician can do a great deal.

But more diseases defy herbs than yield to them. So there is the second set of weapons we physicians use. Call them, if you like, mental treatment. They consist of persuading a patient first of all that he is better than he thinks he is, then that he is much better still, then that he is so much better that he is not ill at all, and finally that he is completely cured and will not become ill in that way again. (If you are thinking that this is how your own disease was ended three years ago, you are so little right that you are mostly wrong. That jug of boiling water from which you inhaled the steam—you will remember it because you hated it so much—well, there was in the water a certain preparation of herbs.) If you had to find a name for this treatment perhaps you might call it Suggestion, for it consists in suggesting to a patient what you want him to believe until he really does believe it, and then, probably, he is healed of his sick mind or his fear. For this to be successful, the physician must see behind the façade of a patient's talk what it is really both expressing and concealing. He must do this with sympathetic understanding, and the patient must completely trust his physician. Then, very often, the patient's lost confidence, which causes so many diseases, can be restored to him again, and then the disease vanishes.

But there are so many diseases which neither of these weapons can touch. They are those in which something goes suddenly wrong inside a patient's body, a stoppage in the human drainage system for instance, or a clot of blood in an artery, or some muscular defect which slows the motion of the heart, or that mysterious disease caused by the cells in a vital organ suddenly becoming malignant. Physicians know what these diseases are, but we are helpless against them. A patient dies, and we are sure that one of these conditions has killed him, but until his dead body has been dissected we cannot tell which of them it was. Then, when it is too late, we know. But you cannot take a knife and dissect a living body. The physician's knife can deal with a cyst or a boil on the outside of the body, but nothing more. A child swallows a cherry stone, and it lodges fast in his throat, and that child dies. It happens every day, and it is heart-rending, but there is nothing we can do. Against all these things, herbs and mental treatment are useless.

You see, then, how much of a doctor's time perforce be spent in sadly recognising how helpless he is. Yet all the time while I am walking in the streets of Antioch, and when I am looking at some poor sufferer stretched feebly upon a bed I have a feeling deep in my heart that I should not and need not be so aware of how little can be done to help and save her. It ought to be possible to do so much more. Our modern knowledge of the body and the mind is less than we physicians would wish it to be, but it is far more than the layman suspects. It is enough to give healing to many more patients than any of us can heal now, if we had that sense of confident power over the evil which in one way or another lurks at the root

of so much physical suffering. To see in a single day, as I
often do, a young child die because it has swallowed a pin
which dropped to the floor from its mother's dress, a woman so
ravaged by the pox that she is growing blind and mad, an old
man slowly dying because for years he had been too poor to
get enough to eat—these things rend the heart. And they do
this not only because they outrage one's sense of pity, but also
and more because they mock the exactness and care of the
modern physician's training, and the nobility of purpose which
that training drills into him.

We are taught our business, as you know, in medical schools;
and I myself was trained in the School at Athens which is
perhaps the best of them all. There they show us skilfully
how the human body is put together, how each part of it
works, how it co-operates with all the other parts, how and
why each part of it may go wrong and become diseased, and
what to do when this has happened. We are taught very
exactly the powers and properties of healing herbs and roots.
We are trained to keep very careful notes of the symptoms of
each disease we meet, of the course it takes, and of how we
have cured it, if and when we are successful. They even teach
us the art of making notes by a secret kind of very swift
writing, in which a single stroke of a stylus or a hurriedly
drawn hieroglyphic will express for us the meaning of quite a
long sentence of ordinary writing. All this may take as long
as three years, and we may not practise our art with the
school's blessing until our teachers give us letters to certify that
we have properly learned our trade. Then when all is at last
done, we are called together and we solemnly and publicly
bind ourselves by reciting the noble oath of Hippocrates, the
father of all our tribe. Perhaps you do not know this oath, so I
write it down for you to read since I am pledged to it, and it
forms the basis of all my life and is the great rule I must keep
or be dishonoured.

I swear by Apollo the Healer, the Aesculapius, and Hygieia, and Panacea; and I call all gods and goddesses to witness, that I will, according to my power and judgement, make good this oath and covenant that I sign. I will use all ways of medical treatment that shall be for the advantage of the sufferers, according to my power and judgement, and will protect them from injury and injustice. Nor will I give to any man, though I be asked to give it, any deadly drug, nor will I consent that it should be given. But purely and holily I will keep guard over my life and my art.

And into whatever houses I enter, I will enter into them for the benefit of the sufferers, departing from all wilful injustice and destructiveness, and all lustful works, on bodies, male and female, free and slaves. And whatever in practice I see or hear, or even outside practice, which it is not right should be told abroad, I will be silent, counting as unsaid what was said.

Therefore to me, accomplishing this oath and not confounding it, may there be enjoyment of life and art, being in good repute among all men for ever and ever: but to me, transgressing and perjured, the contrary.

This oath is good, but its authorities are feeble. Apollo, Hygieia, Panacea—the scroll of names rings as one reads them, but it is not to their authority that I am bound. No educated man believes that these old gods exist. You do not believe in them—nor do I. They can exercise no authority over us, and we can have no loyalty to them. Nor can I find in myself any faith in all these new oracles of the mystery religions, though it is true that many of my brother physicians resort to them more and more. I think indeed that the decline of the old gods and the feebleness of the new is not the least of the symptoms of our modern sickness of society. If we are citizens of a world which is losing its nerve, it is because to so many of us the heavens seem empty and untenanted. There is for me no god with power to help or authority to order me. When I knock at the door of a house where there is dangerous sickness, I carry with me my knowledge and my compassion, and they are not enough. I do not utter a prayer to Apollo to help me. There is no god to whom I would instinctively pray at such a moment with any real belief that he will or can do for my patient what I know that I cannot do for him myself.

And what, do you ask, is this? Yes, it is more than making him well. I long to make him whole, to cure the whole disharmony of which his fever or his rheumatism is but a symptom, so that he may have again his full chance to lead the Good Life, which is the complete life, the whole of life harmonised in the service of a worthy aim, and not merely the life of the Golden Mean which Aristotle used to teach. That is the promise of the Oath of Hippocrates. But it begins by pointing the physician to gods which are no gods, and it puts at his disposal no powers and no knowledge not already his own. And these are never enough. For me there can be no content until outside every house I enter I can pray to a God who cares that the woman inside lies sick and can act through the physician to cure her and make her whole. Meanwhile I have my duty to do, and I do it, but it satisfies neither myself nor my patients.

Theophilus to Silvanus   ROME
                                                          A.D. 31

YOU will think ill of me for my long silence, though
   remember that I too have had nought but silence from
you for the same period of more than a year. Let us resume
our letters, the pledges of friendship. The new safe, sure, and
regular postal service, organised by the Emperor to cover the
farthest limits of the world, can carry them from Jerusalem to
Rome at small cost. For some time this service has as a matter
of fact been carrying frequent letters from this office to both
Caesarea and Jerusalem. But all these have been official letters,
concerned with the case of our unhappy and stupid procurator
Pontius, who is now here in Rome and making my life
difficult by haunting my office and begging for the work he
will never be given again. He is very miserable, and full of
resentment, but also he is very lucky. Did he but know it, it
is only the pleading and the high reputation of Procula his
wife which has saved him from banishment or worse. She
told me that she tried her utmost to save him from bringing
Roman justice into contempt by his weakness in the case of
that man Jesus. But he is the sort of man who thinks that
every woman is intellectually inferior to every man, and when
the woman is Procula and the man is Pontius, his conceit is so
abysmal as to be almost comic. I must not write more about
this affair, but what does puzzle me is how such a man as this
Jesus seems to have been can have made so deep and lasting an
impression on a woman with the power of mind and judgement
of Procula. Oh yes, I know as well as she and you that he was
innocent of the offences charged against him. Even Pontius
knew that. But beyond his innocence and the injustice of his

fate, what was in him to have such an influence on one of the
wisest and noblest women of our time?

But it is not of Pontius, or Jesus, or even of Procula that I
want to write to you, my dear Silvanus. I write to ask for
your help for a friend—after yourself, the oldest and dearest
of all my friends—Luke, the physician of Antioch. He it is
who, as I told you three years ago, gave me back my health
when my despair had brought me to the very edge of killing
myself. You said then that you had never met him, and if he
had met you since then I think he would have told me in one
of his letters, for to both of you the encounter would have
been.an event making golden the day it happened. But now I
hope you will soon meet him, for he greatly needs help, and
help of the sort you can best give, and which I ask you to give
for the sake of our long friendship. Antioch is not so very
distant from Jerusalem, and far nearer than Rome; and your
journey will be rewarded for Luke is one of those people
whom it is always an enrichment to have known.

He is so tall and so broad, as to be physically an exceptionally
large man. A friend of his once described him as a positive
bull of a man with a kind intelligent face. He is slow and
deliberate, and yet active in movement and in speech; and he
carries with him about his work the benignant and calm
silence of the born listener. He works hard but unhurriedly.
What spare time he gives himself he occupies by writing
poetry and painting pictures. There is in him all the grace and
balanced strength of the man who lives his life to the full in
all its parts, and keeps each power he has under the control of
the harmony of all.

He lives in the Street of the Herbalists, and from there he
practises his physician's art. He is a great physician. I can
testify to that, for with me he succeeded where so many
others had failed. But there is other testimony to his greatness
than my own. I get many letters from Antioch, as you would

expect from its great importance in the Empire. They come from men on the procurator's staff, from our legionaries, from merchants and ships' captains, and many others, and in quite a number of them there is some mention of the 'famous physician of Antioch'. They have but to mention his name, and at once an air of devoted gratitude comes over their sentences. It is not only or chiefly his great skill which moves them all. More than that, it is of his patience, his strong compassion, and his extraordinary sensitiveness of understanding that they all speak with astonishment and praise. But if he is kind he can also be firm. He has that kind of gentle persistence which cloaks an element of steel lying deep in the hidden recesses of his nature. His patients obey his orders even though they do not welcome them. So at least they tell me, and I can believe it for so it was in my case. What he made me do was most unpleasing. I revolted against it over and over again, but I did it. Then they recognise in him another and a still rarer quality, his repudiation of any particular obligation owed by him to high position or great wealth. All human beings are alike to him, and none more important or worthier of his attention than another. But though in his eyes all men and women are equal in his affections, it is at a high value not a low one that he rates this equality. The slave is the prince to him, and the prince remains what he is, not changing places with the slave. His most fully cared for patients are those who are most sick, and it is all one to him whether the patient is a prostitute in a dockside stew, a slave tugging an oar on one of our galleys, or the Roman procurator's secretary. Indeed of him it is almost true to say that he thinks more highly of the poor than the rich for he is always reminding himself of how little chance they have had, and he has an even quicker sympathy for women than men. And all my correspondents say that his own personal life is consistent with these tendencies so prominent in his professional life.

One thing about him which impresses and puzzles his friends and patients is his indifference to wealth, and his real anger that money should have so much power over all human life. He once said something to me which I have never forgotten— 'The symbol of authority ought to be a kiss, not a coin'. His patients go to see him. He lances their boils, or concocts a brew of herbs for their fever, or spends hours and hours in talk with them to heal their minds. Then they ask him what they must pay. At once he seems embarrassed and answers, 'Whatever seems right and fair to you. There is a bowl on that table. Put in it as much or as little you as like'. Then he abruptly changes conversation. Perhaps it is to the credit of our human nature that no one ever does go without making his offering in Luke's bowl.

Now this is the man who is in danger of himself becoming sick in mind. I do not mean that he may go mad. He will not do that for he is too practical. But already he has this gentle melancholy, which can so easily and so unnoticed become disillusion. The disillusion, in turn, grows into despair; and the despair develops into a permanent state of contented dejection. It will be simplest for me to send you in strict confidence his last letter to me. One of my copyists here has transcribed it, and I will add it to this letter before I close and send it.

I know that I understand it because I have seen this apparently causeless unhappiness in others, and I have to fight it in myself. I believe that you will understand it because you hinted in a letter of yours some years ago that you were finding it difficult to see what value or real purpose there was in your life. A very busy life, you said, but achieving—what? So it is with Luke. Do you not think it a remarkable and significant fact that we three men should all independently be asking questions about the purpose of life that none of us can answer? Is it not strange that we all know that our peace of mind depends on our being able to find an answer? For look at us! I am a senior civil servant; Luke is a successful and beloved physician; and you are both a famous lawyer and a fine poet. We have position, authority, sufficient wealth, and have realised most of our youthful ambitions. We have been fortunate far beyond most men of our time. We enjoy every good thing the Roman Empire has to give, and that is much—peace, security, health, civilisation, control of our own time, and enough education for us to be able to appreciate it all. No previous generation in the history of the world could claim so much or live so well. Rightly is Rome called great. She has given peace and law and justice to the whole world, and we three men have at our command all the finest fruits of this immense achievement.

And yet, ingrates that we are, these fruits taste sour in our mouths. We taste daily what our ancestors would have given their eyes to glimpse occasionally, and it does not satisfy or nourish us. Having almost everything the mind of man can desire, we still yearn for and covet—what? The gods, if gods there be, to teach us the answer to the riddle of life? Is this world become so tame and ordinary to us that we discontentedly seek another? Rhetoric perhaps, but truth too. We know it is so with all three of us, and with many, many others too. Luke, as you will see when you read the copy of his letter, blames it all on the Gods which are no Gods worth worshipping, on the stoic and epicurean surrogates for religion which offer nothing to worship, on the novel craze for esoteric mystery hunting which ministers only to human curiosity and gives man no power. We are surrounded on every side by scores of religions. They all have their temples, priesthoods, rituals and votaries; but none of them tells me of a god in whom I would take the trouble to believe. It is for lack of a true and worthy religion that the springs of the world are drying up.

I have heard vague rumours that you believe yourself to have found some new spiritual hope, and that it is in some way connected with this Jesus whom Pontius betrayed Roman justice by crucifying. To me, this seems a little bizarre and extravagant, but it may be that this rumour of you is false. Absurd as such a faith may sound to me, I think I should be a little disappointed if rumour wholly lied. A Roman official should be the last to throw stones, for in his heart he knows well that Rome gives peace without heroes, and sanitation without love.

Do your best for Luke. Give him a hero to worship and a cause to serve. Yours would be better than none.

LETTER FOUR

Silvanus to Luke   JERUSALEM
                                                         A.D. 31

IT is possible that before this you may have heard my name
from His Excellency Theophilus of Rome, a friend of
many years' standing to both of us. But I have never, I think,
had the pleasure of meeting you, though I hope it may not be
long before this happens. I am venturing to write to introduce
myself now because that is what Theophilus has asked me to do.
Yesterday a long letter from him arrived here, and in it he
asked (no, he begged) me to get into touch with you, to give
you his greetings, and, if I may, to try to do something else
as well.

Now this mission which he thrusts on me is more delicate
and even embarrassing than he seems to think. It is that I, a
Jewish lawyer, should intrude upon you, a famous Greek
physician of Antioch, and make an offer to be of any service
to you in the need he says you have. Indeed and indeed I will
try to be of what service I can to any son of God, and of
whatever race or nation—and how much more to the friend
of a friend. For I am a follower of the Jesus of Nazareth of
whom you have probably heard, who came to crown the
whole long tale of our Jewish history, and, more than that,
to be the hope of every nation on earth. Almost his last command was that his followers should seek for other followers
among all the nations. The Movement which he inaugurated
started among the Jews but it is not for us alone. Already it is
spreading among our hereditary enemies, the Samaritans, and
from them again to most of the cities of Asia Minor, Antioch
of Syria being the chief among them. You can find his people
in your own city, and perhaps you have already done this.

I write all this because I know so well how great is the damage we Jews have done to our reputation by our chronic racial exclusiveness, and I fear that it is but natural for a Greek who receives a letter from a Jew to read it with reserve and suspicion. But though this exclusiveness, this sense that we alone are the chosen people of God, has for century after century been bred into the bones of the Jews, it is also true that this old curse is at last broken at least in such of the Jews who are followers of Jesus. We are to proclaim him as the lord of all nations equally, and we preach a religion of universal brotherhood within which all the old barriers of race and nationhood are broken down. So it is as a friend of Theophilus who has commanded me, and as a follower of the Lord Jesus, and not only as a Jew that I am writing.

Nevertheless, a stranger who ventures to offer to be of help to a stranger must perforce walk delicately. I offer, but it is for you to accept or to refuse, and for me to abide without further question by your decision. The freedom of another man must be as precious to me as my own.

Theophilus writes that he has asked me rather than some other man to offer you this service, because your particular difficulty is his difficulty, and for a long time was also mine. So he believes that I shall know exactly what this sense of life's futility feels like, and how devastating and even paralysing it can be. Indeed I know all about it. To be convinced that all human effort is futile, that life has no goal and our work but little purpose is to walk through the world under a black cloud. One goes on with the motions of living and persists with the fulfilment of duty, but these bring no peace and life becomes boring and dreary. Soon I found myself spending long hours of every day sitting in a corner and staring at nothing. All life became unutterably wearisome.

I describe what my own state was but not, I profoundly hope, what your state has yet become. Yet it is to this and

worse than this that it can lead. I say that this was my state.
It is not my state now. In the words of one of our old Jewish
psalms, 'The snare was broken and I was delivered'. That is
the point. We cannot break the snare ourselves or free ourselves. It has to be broken for us from outside by someone
other than ourselves, and we have to be set free by another.
That other may be God, or someone who is specially inspired
by God, or it may be some friend whom one completely
trusts. But it is never ourselves. Once we are in this snare we
are impotent. Our strength then must be another's strength,
for though we long for it we have none. At the time of my
mental suffering I believed my Jewish religion. I still do. But it
could not save me. The power to save was in it but I could
not lay hold of it because I had missed the clue. It was only
when I saw with my own eyes that Jesus was carefully and
exactly fulfilling all the promises of our old prophets in the
scriptures, that I slowly began to realise that he must himself
be the fulfilment of the hope of our race. Then I met him, and
talked with him, and he seemed to have all the secrets of hope
in him and all the strength of a not less than divine authority.
I did not need to describe my trouble to him. He knew it all by
his own unerring and instinctive insight. And he forgave me, and
set me free. Someday, perhaps, I will tell you the details of
that talk which saved me, but it was as though life began all
over again for me on that sunny morning on the mountain.
So I became a follower of his; and now I am trying to pay a
tiny fraction of my endless debt to him by writing to you of
the things which belong to my peace.

Your own peace can come in the same way, but whether
by that way or some other I pray that it comes speedily. The
whole point is that there are some devils which cannot be cast
out of man but by a divine, supernatural, and spiritual power—
in fact by the power of God, and it is nothing less than God
that we followers believe that Jesus was and is. And if God,

then God, and every power of God for us all, Greeks, Romans,
Jews alike and equally. To this God, the only true God, in
Jesus I commend you.

I will come to you in Antioch as soon as I may if you will
allow me. For the next few months I have things to do in
Jerusalem which I must not leave. After that I can make myself
free to come if you ask me. It will be all the more interesting
as I have never been in Antioch before. But meanwhile, I
wonder if you would see a friend of mine in Antioch who I
believe could help. You may already know him, Nicholas, a
coppersmith, who lives in a house near the market place.
He too is a Jew, and belongs to what we call 'The Dispersion',
that is, the Jews who live abroad. He is also a follower of
Jesus and now a prominent one for in the earliest days he was
one of a small group of men appointed to assist the rulers of
the Church, the twelve men whom Jesus himself chose and
whom we call Apostles. The difference is that the Apostles
undertake most of the travelling and preaching while the
Deacons, as we call them, do the ordinary day by day admini-
stration of the church where they live. Nicholas is our deacon
at Antioch and so he is usually to be found there. You will,
I hope and think, take to him, no one knows him and then
fails to love him. Nevertheless, I plan to come to Antioch
myself as soon as I can, for it would be a joy and privilege to
me to meet so close a friend of Theophilus. And so I commend
you to the healing power of the God of all Gods and to his
devoted Servant Nicholas of Antioch.

LETTER FIVE

Nicholas to Silvanus ANTIOCH
A.D. 32

(I, Persis, a public scribe and copyist and brother in Christ, write
this at the dictation of our brother Nicholas, who says his hands
are better able to beat a copper vase than to wield a pen.)

I HAD begun to say Most Honoured Sir, which seems only
right and respectful from a coppersmith to a great lawyer
such as Your Honour is, but Persis says that now we are both
followers of Jesus our Lord, I ought to begin with 'Dearest
Brother'. So I do as he tells me, but truly, Sir, it doesn't look
quite right somehow.

I send my respectful greetings and beg to state that I have
carried out your orders. There was no difficulty for the great
physician Luke, grand man that he is, is well known to all my
family, for he has long been our doctor. Only three months
ago he brought our youngest baby into the world, a dear little
girl and very bonny and well. We have called her Miriam.
When we told him that she was to be brought up to be one
more of the followers of our dear Lord, and would soon be
taken to be baptised in his name, he was so interested, and
asked all manner of questions, and we explained as best we
could, not, as you know Sir, or should I say, brother, being
scholars but ordinary labouring people. But he seemed to
understand most of it somehow in that way he has of guessing
your thoughts before you speak them. And he seemed so
interested too, but then he always is interested in every little
detail of his patients whom he always seems to think of as his
friends, whether they are great rabbis or Roman Officials or
just working folk like my dear wife Naomi and me. When

we told him all about the baptism, he listened and then he sighed, and then he said, 'Would little Miriam take another blessing from one who is a seeker not a follower, but is very fond of her?', and he put his hands on her small head and blessed her in the names of the first of her friends and of the Great God he didn't know but hoped to find and we thought it was so nice and kind of him.

(I do hope, Sir, we did no wrong, I mean, in allowing a heathen physician to do it for after all that's what he is, though it seems peculiar somehow, I mean *him* being a heathen, but it would have been so rude to stop him, and I can't think Jesus our Lord would have wanted us to do that.)

Well, Sir, that talk gave me a chance, as you might say, so when your letter came I asked if I could come to see him soon and he said, 'Yes — for you are the friend who has been sent to me, are you not?' and I said, 'Yes', so I went the next evening and showed him your letter, and he told me some of what you had written to him, but not all of it.

I'm not a man of much education, as you know, honoured brother, and wearing my best clothes made me feel a bit awkward-like even with Luke who always makes me feel natural when he comes to see us at home and I'm in my working shirt and my old leather apron which always seems so much more comfortable and easy, if you understand me. So I expect I was stupid, and though I tried as hard as I could, I really couldn't quite understand what this trouble of his is all about. I mean, he isn't ill in any way, and he hasn't done no sin, not *him*—I'd never believe that—and he's one of the very few men in all Antioch who's got no enemies, and he isn't poor, so it's hard to see just what the matter is. Of course, he isn't a follower, and I think he'd like to be but something seems to hold him back. So I remembered how our dear Lord always listened so patient and quiet to everything people had to say about their troubles, and then when they had told him how they thought about them he would tell them so gently and kindly and firmly how they ought to think about them, and they always went away so happy, and sort of set free. I ought to know! That's what Jesus did for me.

I suppose that Luke really wants to be set free too, though I can't think what from. So I told him what Jesus had done for me, and then I said to him that if he would trust him and pray hard, I thought, no, I knew, he would do the same for him too, and then he could be baptised too and be a follower with all the rest of us, and how lovely that would be, and how gladly we would all welcome him.

He looked a little puzzled and sad, and said that he really wanted that more than anything else. 'You followers', he said, 'have all got such a strong purpose in your lives, and you all seem to love each other so much'. So I said that that was true, but that we didn't love each other any more than we all loved him; and, indeed, honoured brother, that is true. Luke is the one physician in Antioch whom everybody loves. I mean, you can't help loving him; nobody could, and he is much the best-known man in the whole city. You don't have to be a follower of Jesus to love Luke, for you'd have to be a son of Beelzebub not to. But then, Sir, you know that better than I do.

Well then he went on to say that he really couldn't give his life to a man he knew nothing about. So I told him how he was crucified and God had raised him from death, and how he forgives us all our sins whenever we're sorry and is present with us always. He said he couldn't believe he had risen from the dead, for dead people don't do that sort of thing; and I said 'No, I know they don't but he did, and I know he did, because I saw him myself', but he shook his head.

So I told him how our scriptures had foretold that all this must happen to the Messiah, and he said a little sharply, '*Jewish* scripture', and I said, 'Yes, but read them and see'. So to cut a long story short (and Persis says that if I go on much longer he will have to charge me double for writing this) I said, would he read the Scriptures if I could get him a Greek copy, for I knew that our brother Issachar had one and would be certain to lend it to Luke if I asked him and he said he would. So I went at once round to Issachar and asked him if he would lend it to Luke and he agreed. So now he's got it and in a day or two Issachar who is a real scholar, he can write Greek as well as read it! is going to see him to ask if he can help by explaining what our prophets meant. I hope, Sir, you think I did right.

Before I close, the followers here are worried about what has been happening in Jerusalem. It isn't poor Stephen's death. He was made a deacon along with me, and he always was a little violent in his talk when he got roused, as you know, Sir, and I suppose when he made that speech to the Pharisees he must have let them have it good and proper, as the saying is, though we here haven't heard what he did say, that is, except for his last words. Well, he's a martyr in heaven now, and brother Manaen says we must rejoice over him and I do, but, oh Sir, I can't forget those rocks they threw at him, and in my dreams I hear them thud on his poor head. But they tell me he forgave them, as Jesus forgave those poor ignorant Roman soldiers, and that he smiled and called out to the Master when he died, so I suppose it must be all right. But we are getting a lot of new followers from Jerusalem in our church here, Jews, Greeks, Cypriots and all sorts, and they say that it isn't safe to be a follower in Jerusalem now, and that when the High Priest finds one he puts him in prison as soon as look at him. Can you tell us, Sir, is this true? And is it going to happen to us here too?

Well, honourable brother, I must close at last, and I send my respectful greetings and my dear wife's too, praying that our dear Lord will bless us all, and show himself to Luke so that he joins us in the church.

LETTER SIX

DEAR old Nicholas, whom you sent to me, has discharged his mission. He did it after his own manner, his warm heart, his perpetual consciousness of 'being no scholar as you know, sir', and his delicate hesitancy of speech on matters so nearly private and intimate, all struggling together within him. He hesitated and he stammered, and for a time it was embarrassing for us both until I at last managed to put him at his ease. Then he forgot himself, forgot too that he was wearing his new clothes (why is it that new clothes tie people's tongues in knots? they nearly always do), and he spoke freely as his heart dictated. Though he really had no idea at all of the nature of the chronic discontent which has been afflicting me, his instinct led him rightly to speak chiefly of his own experience as a follower of Jesus, and when he left me I felt better than I had done for many months past.

Probably you already know all this for he said he would make some report to you. So I really need not have written the first paragraph of this letter. But it is a joy even to think of Nicholas and a pleasure to write about him, for this recalls to me his beaming face, his honest eyes, and all his ways of kindliness and peace. He is the sort of man whom everyone inevitably calls 'Dear Old Nicholas', though indeed he is not very old. But he has a mature steadiness about him, and being himself essentially serene and uncomplicated, and wholly without ambition for position or greed for money, he carries about with him a blessing wherever he goes, and is essentially unaware of it himself. The group of followers of Jesus here has many men and women in it of wealth, education, and high

social position, but there is none of them who is not content
that Nicholas should be one of their chief leaders, their deacon
as I think you call him. In his presence their sense of class drops
from them; and one of the things which most deeply impresses
me about them all is how they let his simple but profound
humility call forth from them the same humility which, by
nature, they find so much harder than he does. If it is the
business of the deacon to hold the community together and
keep them happy and in true fellowship with one another,
Nicholas does this much better than any of the others would
do, and they know it.

Better, for instance, than Issachar, who also came to see me
at Nicholas' request, carrying with him a Greek copy of your
Jewish scriptures. You will want me to write for you my
impressions of it, and this I will do presently. But I want to
give you a picture of Issachar too, to illustrate the astonishing
variety of the material of which the group of followers of
Jesus here is composed. Issachar is entirely different from
Nicholas. He is a young and brilliant lawyer, very wealthy,
very successful, and—forgive me!—very, very self-consciously
Jewish. He is certainly a disciple of Jesus, but if the fullness of
Jesus' spirit has passed into Nicholas, then Issachar has not
yet been more than damped by its spray. He is inclined to think
that to belong to Jesus it is necessary first to have belonged to
Jewry, and he looks rather askance on the newer type of
follower now in Antioch, who may well be a Greek, a Syrian,
or a Roman. It is as though he thought that they find their
peace too easily, and are escaping the price he has had to pay
for his. Poor man, I am really rather sorry for him. He has a
torment in his belly which gnaws, and he doesn't know it.
Thus when he came to lend me his precious books, he acted
all the time as though he felt it somehow wrong to aid and abet
the reading by a Greek physician of a Jewish holy book. And
when he offered to come later and explain to me what I,

being a Greek, could not be expected to understand for myself, (almost but not quite his very words,) his whole attitude was only just short of aggressiveness. Nevertheless, he will come because Nicholas has asked him, and that is one measure of the worth of Nicholas.

In my leisure time of the last few weeks I have been immersed in the books which Issachar brought. I have not read their every word, but I have ranged widely about them and in many places I have dug deep into them, and I think I understand their general drift of meaning. Reading and pondering them has been a very stimulating experience but also an oddly incongruous one. The incongruity lies in reading books like these in a place like this. They bring Jerusalem into Antioch, and though but few miles separate them, were ever two cities in the same world so wildly different?

These books come out of the hot and dusty stew of hate which is Jerusalem. They tell of murdered Kings and blood-thirsty Queens, of the massacre of whole provinces and the long mass captivity of the very nation which lived and wrote them. Asserting, as they do over and over again, that this nation is divinely separated and privileged above all others, being chosen by God in a sense true of no other nation, they breathe the essence of proud racial exclusiveness, yet they narrate a national history more lamentable and disastrous than that of any other nation which makes no claim to be the first, no, the only favourite of God. Not only are these books filled with cruelty and horror, but they mirror a people who have no talent for civilisation and no sense of its value, and they depict a life which is nasty and short, and wholly insecure even while it lasts. Their sense of values, too, is strange to the point of madness. If there is a trivial detail of life and its arrangement, such as, for example, the shape of a priest's vestment, to this these writers will devote page after page of exact description. For the murder of a king one line is enough. Never was more lavish description of the outside of a temple, but of what goes on inside it, the very thing for which the temple was built, they have virtually nothing to say. To read them is like living for centuries in an atmosphere hot and strained, savage and tense, with hardly a loophole to let in a cool and lucid wind to clear the room of thunder.

And these are the books which I sit in my room in Antioch and read—in Antioch, the exact opposite of the whole life they describe and the spirit they breathe. For Antioch is a very clean city, a most comfortable city, a city of light and water. At night the streets are lit by hanging lamps. Every street has its public baths and washhouses; every house has fresh water running through it. Every street, every building is clean and gleaming. No dust lies long here, no great heat scorches us, no intensity of hate spoils life for us. It is quite true, I think, that this is the most beautiful city in the world to see, and the pleasantest and easiest to live in. You will not doubt it when you sit in the cypress groves of the Daphne Gardens, or walk from the walled town through the valley of the Orontes river, where the beautiful new villas of the wealthy are being built, to the Daphne, at the gate of which stands the magnificent Temple of Apollo. We have schools, public buildings, baths, theatres, and all of them lavish and costly; and we have the wealth to provide all these things. In Damascus they have their famous 'Street Called Straight'. I once saw it. But our long straight street, the Prada, is far finer. It runs for four and a half miles, and has a covered colonnade of shops on either side, and the roadway is wide enough to take four carriages abreast. And life here is so peaceful, so secure, so gay, so civilised. I am in a very different world from the Jerusalem of these scriptures of yours. No one here would dream of murdering a king. They would never take the trouble for they would never care enough.

Oh, it is easy enough to live well here if you have a little

money. You need not fear, nor suffer, nor feel anguish or
dread. A child could learn the technique of living easily. All
this is true of Antioch—and it sickens and angers me. It is not
that I revolt against civic order and cleanliness. I am a Greek
and as such a love of the cool lucidity of an ordered life was
bred into my bones. I would not choose a tense seething
forcing-house of explosive passion like Jerusalem to live in.
But there is this to be said for Jerusalem (if these holy books
genuinely capture its spirit), that at least these citizens of yours
do care for something outside themselves, and care enough
to plot for it, kill for it, and die for it. In Antioch all too few
care much for anything, and therefore few people are cared
for much by anyone. There seems to be a quite shocking
absence of social and even personal compassion. The external
arrangements of the life of Antiochans are so good that it seems
to be taken for granted that human suffering ought not to exist.
Where it does nevertheless and obstinately exist, it is as though
people regarded it as a kind of unseemly outrage upon the
orderliness of life, an unspoken threat to their light-minded
serenity, and so they drive it from their minds and forget.
They repudiate sympathy, and therefore are without any
driving force of compassion.

So it is that the spirit of Antioch is a vast inconsistency.
We have everything and create nothing. We have no poets
and no philosophers, but we specialise in parodists, and the
kind of stage play which is clever, brittle, and heartless. Our
stage abounds with clowns and comedians. They are as accomplished as they are plentiful. In fact our native clowns dominate
the stages of Rome itself, where Antioch is known to be the
home of great buildings, incomparable natural beauty, and
gay light-minded citizens. But if this light-mindedness, with
its quick wit and brittle gaiety is superficially attractive, perpetual levity is a metal which has a dark under-side, and it is
this side of it which we physicians see. There is great cruelty.

It is not wreaked on people by bloody minded tyrants, for that foul brood does not flourish in Antioch. It comes precisely through the unheeding, uncaring nature of a light-minded people, who, having no particular moral standards, deny themselves heights to aspire to or depths to sink to. They condemn nothing and praise nothing and believe in nothing. As a natural consequence they are most monstrously cruel, for they do not even believe in cruelty.

The cruelty is unintended, but, Silvanus, it is real. The Temple of Apollo has its Court of Prostitutes and its services are such as excite worshippers to use it. They do, and you know what the end of the prostitute is. So do these people, but they prefer not to know. These wretched women die in their hovels and I rage helplessly by their bedsides. By the time they are forty, the glass blowers are apt to contract a disease of the lungs, which kills them slowly with a kind of creeping paralysis. One of these sat silently for many days at the gate of the beautiful new villa which the merchant who had employed him had built out of the profits of that man's rotting body. He was indeed a loathsome sight towards the end. When his employer came out he struggled to rise to his feet and beg for his help. But he was never noticed, never acknowledged. The merchant sprinkled himself with aromatic scent, crossed the road, and went on his way chatting gaily with his rich friends. These things happen here every day. No one condemns them. No one bothers about them. No remedy exists for them.

Thus, living in this lovely city of little men, I, you will easily believe, am being deeply and powerfully impressed by your Jewish scripture. I have already said how essentially savage they seem to me. Yet, even in their most bestial excesses, they tell of a nation which cares incessantly and profoundly for its nationhood and its religion. It follows that they are also full of compassion and tenderness. In the whole of Greek literature is there a phrase so wonderfully pitiful as the one about 'Rachel mourning for her children, and would not be comforted because they are not', or the scene where David the King is told of his son Absolom's death? Our story of the tears of Niobe is pallid in comparison.

I must not weary you with too much detail. That can keep until the day—may it come soon—when we can talk together. But I think I must tell you now, albeit briefly, of the strongest impressions I have received from your Jewish scriptures. The first is their faith that the world is so ordered that, in spite of all appearances, the weak are in the long run stronger than the mighty, if they are humble enough and sensitive enough to count on a spiritual strength greater than their own. The shepherd boy with his sling slays the giant. The lion lies down with the ox when a little child leads them. And there are other illustrations of the same thing.

Then, and really arising from that, there is that astonishing passage in Isaiah, where he foretells the coming of the Great Deliverer, who is to be nothing less than the crown and vindication of the whole calamitous tale of Jewish history, and then insists that he will be so scarred and stained and filled with grief that he cannot be recognised for what he is, and so is bound to be rejected by the very nation he comes to save. All that the disciples here have told me about the life and death of Jesus shows how exactly he fulfilled this prophecy, written hundreds of years before he was born. The veriest heathen among readers must bow in wonder before a passage like that, and I cannot doubt that the divine spirit himself at that point taught Isaiah what to write.

But over and above all this, there is the unwearied determination of the Jews to make the whole range of their national life revolve round the idea that they had of God, so that it all takes its colour from him. When they thought of him as vengeful and cruel they themselves became vengeful and cruel.

When they thought of him as the pivot of social order, they at once produced the Mosaic code of law. When they began to picture him as compassionate, they came at last to value pity and tenderness. But throughout this history with its changing and often contradictory conceptions of what qualities were to be found in God, there was one basic quality they always seemed to recognise in him—his energy. The God one finds in these books is a God who is always in action, always doing things. In fact he is a God in whom it is always worth while to believe. Besides that, the total failure of the Jews in these books to see any point or purpose in civilisation is but a little thing.

Almost these books persuade one. The spirit I find among, and the welcome I receive from the followers of Jesus persuade me. The sickening sham religion of Antioch persuades me. My weariness of the dignified but hopeless religion I once had persuades me. I knew I must worship or become less than human. But the only kind of deity in whom I could honestly believe was unknown and unknowable. He, I supposed, remained eternally unaware of the worship offered, as also of the existence of him who offered it. I could conceive such a God, and I could bow before him in adoration. But I could not pray to him.

The point to which all these spiritual futilities have brought me is that I am a probationary member of the church here. I have not yet asked for baptism but I am being prepared for it. There is much to learn and far to go, but already I have a cause to serve, a hero to worship, and a community of loving spirits to support me, and I am happier than I have been for years. I owe most of it to you. Come and visit me here as soon as you can, and let me thank you.

Issachar to James the Elder   ANTIOCH
                                                       A.D. 35

BECAUSE I am perturbed and apprehensive about the lax
way the affairs of the church here in Antioch are being
conducted, I have thought it my duty to write to you, the
senior member of our mother church of Jerusalem, to lay
before you the facts which I think you do not know, and to
ask you to give me your ruling upon them.

Our Lord Jesus came from the most high God to save his
own people, the Jews. They were Jewish scriptures to which
he appealed, Jewish prophecies which he scrupulously fulfilled,
the Jewish Law of Moses which he reformed and obeyed. It
is true that he dealt mercifully with many Gentiles, Samaritans,
Roman soldiers, and others. He even seemed to like them.
He certainly never avoided them. This fact about his mission,
was, as you know, a stumbling block to many of us who had
been educated in the great Law Schools of Judea, and perhaps
some of us would never have become his disciples had we not
seen how shamefully our own custodians and interpreters of
the Law themselves broke it in letter and spirit in all their
dealings with him. But the terrible fact of his trial and crucifixion accuses not the Law itself but its unworthy guardians.
The Law still stands, renewed and refounded in the Messiah,
and its compulsions stand too and are of obligation upon all
who are the disciples of Jesus.

The Law and the Prophets, our scriptures say, were given
to the Jewish nation to equip us to fulfil our ancient destiny to
bear the divine name of the most high God to every nation in
the world. It is we who are the Chosen People, we who are
ordered to carry the missionary burden. Did Jesus ever say

otherwise? We know he did not. Before he came to us our
foreign Jews were members of the Dispersion. They were
obedient to the Law and members of our national mission.
They were not made Gentiles by living abroad. What Jesus
has now done is simply to extend this same Jewish principle
by reaching out to the Gentile nations through such of the
Gentiles as become his disciples. But it is a Jewish principle still,
and it is a Jewish church he has founded. We welcome gladly
our Gentile converts and treat them as honoured brothers
provided that they first acknowledge themselves bound by the
requirements of our Law. But every man, of whatever nation,
who wishes to be a disciple of Jesus must be what he was, a
Jew first of all. We have all had to pay a heavy price for our
discipleship. Their price is lighter, but they must pay it.

That is exactly what is not happening here. Since the stoning
of our brother Stephen (another shameless breach of our Law)
the church in Antioch has become the refuge not only of Jewish
disciples fleeing from persecution, but of many of their Gentile
friends. We now have among our members Greeks, Cypriots,
Syrians, and Romans. They ask daily for baptism, but all that
is asked of them is to acknowledge publicly that Jesus Christ
is the Lord. There is not a word about obedience to our Law,
not a word about abstaining from food unlawful for Jews,
not a word about the circumcision of the males. They are
turning our Jewish church into little better than a Gentile
temple. I have protested to our deacon Nicholas, and all he
does is to smile and tell me not to be unkind. I have protested
to them, and they take no notice of me. They break the
Sabbath, they eat what they like, they refuse to come to our
synagogue, saying that the worship of the church is enough
for them. They make all the discipline of our disciples impossible, and they dishonour our nation by refusing to become
part of it.

Nicholas is a most lovable man, but he is far too weak and

easy-going, and he compromises on vital principles for the sake of peace. His latest convert is Luke the physician of whom you may have heard. He is a very worthy man. But he too refuses all loyalty to the Jews, and he has less excuse than most for I let him read my Greek copy of our scriptures, and this it was, so he says, which brought him to Jesus Christ. Yet he disobeys them, saying, if you please, that Moses is nothing to him, and he is claiming what he ought to see is impossible, namely that he can become a Christian (as we are called now in Antioch) without also being a Jew. He has not yet formally asked for baptism, so I may yet be able to persuade him. But I doubt it. He can quote so many other Gentiles who have been let into the church through the back door.

It is all extremely disturbing, and I hear that in Samaria the same thing is happening. How is it possible for us to keep the church pure and disciplined if the Law itself is to be flouted?

James the Elder to Barnabas   JERUSALEM
                                                 A.D. 35

I AM sending and I ask you to read a copy of a letter which came to me a few days ago. It is written by Issachar, one of the ablest of our younger Christian brothers in Antioch. You will think his letter peevish and censorious. So it is, but yet it is his great zeal for our Jewish Law that makes him seem so. Yesterday I read his letter to my brothers, the Apostles of Jesus, and when we had laid it before the Lord in prayer, we decided to ask you to visit Antioch in our name, as our delegate, and then to give us your report on the church there.

Though the Apostles do not wish to pre-judge the issue which Issachar raises, there is no doubt that it is a most important one, and will become more important as time goes on. We must soon give an answer, and because authority in the church is vested in us by the Lord's own ordinance, it is essential that the answer be right. For this we must have the facts, and we want you to gather them for us so far as they can be seen in Antioch, which, after Jerusalem herself, seems to be becoming the most important of all Christian centres.

As we see it, the question Issachar raises is this: Is it the Lord's will that Gentiles should share in the Christian mission to the world on equal terms with the Jews? Or are the Gentiles subordinate to the Jews in their membership of the church? If the former is true, then it must be wrong to ask the Gentiles to prove their loyalty to our Lord in anything other than accepting him publicly as Lord and Saviour. In particular it must be wrong to demand from them obedience to the Jewish obligations to the Law of Moses and the rite of Circumcision. But if the latter is true, then no man may enter the church of

Christ our Saviour unless he first accepts the Law as binding upon him, and submits himself to the rite of Circumcision.

This arose first, though in a different form, in our brother Philip's mission to Samaria, and to them we sent Peter and John as we are now sending you to Antioch. Then there was Peter's story which he brought back from Joppa, how in obedience to a vision from the Holy Ghost he baptised the Roman Centurion Cornelius, how the divine Spirit was poured out on all the Gentiles present, and how he went in and ate with them, which was contrary to the Law. We called him to account but he convinced us that he was only being obedient to a still higher Law than that of Moses. We could not possibly deny any more that it was the will of Jesus our Lord that his redemption should be offered to the Gentiles as well as to the Jews. Accordingly we publicly accepted this, laying it upon the whole Church as an article of faith that God has granted repentance unto life to the Gentiles as well as to the Jews.

Of course Gentiles may be members of the Church. We have repeatedly said this. But on what terms? Every day makes a decision more urgent. Now from Damascus comes the news that our newest, and soon perhaps to be our greatest brother Paul is so vehemently denouncing the Law in every sermon he preaches that his former confederates among the Pharisees here have sworn an oath to assassinate him. We have no confirmation yet of this rumour from Damascus, but it is likely to be true. Whether it is or not, this is the kind of challenge which will be made wherever the church takes root among people part Jewish and part Gentile. We must soon decide. If it is the Lord's will that Gentiles shall be in the church on equal terms with Jews, so be it. But for us Jews it will mean a heavy sacrifice to accept such an equality. Jesus our Lord was a Jew, and all the first Christians were Jews, with centuries of our tradition of separate exclusiveness bred into them. If we must renounce our priority among the nations, then by God's help we will do so, but it is going to mean for us a tremendous uprooting of custom and habit.

You see, dear brother, we must gather all the facts we can before, in obedience to the Holy Ghost, we can make the decision. Will you, then, go to Antioch, and find out what facts lie behind Issachar's letter, and then report to me? Greet all our brethren in the church there. We bestow upon them, and especially upon you, our Apostolic blessing.

IT is more difficult than you think to give you a satisfactory answer to your question, What does it feel like to be a Christian? It is difficult for me because, as it happens, I am not yet fully a member of the church. I have not yet asked for baptism, though I am being instructed in preparation for it. I am still what we call a neophyte—an enquirer—and there are parts of our worship and mysteries at which I may not be present. I have therefore so much still to learn about it all. And it is difficult for you because you do not yet believe that it is only by following this Way and no other that we may hope to come to a knowledge of the truth about life and history and God. I know so well what your attitude to religion is for until very recently it was mine too. There are so many religions. Why should one be nearer to the truth than another? Many dishes are offered and the sensible man takes what he wants from each of them. I can almost hear you say it and I said it too. But it is incontestable fact that through following this Way of Jesus I have been healed or made whole. I was sick in spirit, and all the springs of my being are now renewed. This deliverance I owe to the power of the Lord Christ through his church, and him alone I thank and worship.

But I must not spatter this letter to you with ecstasies which are so foreign to the old Roman manner. If I bore you I might lose your friendship which just because I am becoming a Christian I treasure all the more. You ask me, What does it feel like to be a Christian? Let me obediently try to answer.

First, most important of all, and before everything else there is the sense of overwhelming relief. I came across a phrase for

it in a book of old Jewish religious poems: The snare is broken
and we are delivered. That is exactly what it feels like. My
experience as a physician suggests that at some moment in
their lives most people suddenly feel that they are in a trap, and
cannot escape. This trap of life is not like the gin in which a
farmer takes a coney or a rat, for the jaws of the gin close like a
flash and the prey has no warning and no chance. But from the
snares which trap us in life we could have escaped if we would.
Our willed and chosen frailties of character lead us into them,
but we do not escape while we can for the frailties bring their
pleasures and they are real and immediate, and for a long time
the jaws of the trap draw so slowly together that their movement is almost imperceptible. So we think we still have plenty
of time both for pleasure and for escape. Then one fine day we
suddenly find that the trap has shut behind us. There is still
room to move inside, but steadily and inexorably the area of
our freedom contracts, and we find ourselves pushed into the
last corner of our prison, from which, beat the walls as we may,
there is no escape. It is a most horrible feeling, and the only
way out is if someone else will break down the walls or wrench
open the trap for us. I know of what I speak for I was in that
miserable position, and you know why I was. But now I have
been set free. I cried for help, and with incredible generosity,
God answered my cry, smashed the trap, and set me free. Yes,
I know that you will be murmuring to yourself that you and
Silvanus and my friends here had much to do with it. Indeed
yes, and I thank you from my heart for so generously obeying
the impulse to come to my rescue which God put into your
heart.

The bait in my snare was the indulgence of thinking that
because the world has much obvious evil in it (in Antioch it is
very obvious, believe me), and because one physician acting
alone in the puny strength of his own unaided powers could
do almost nothing to uproot this evil, all human endeavour

was futile and life was hardly worth living. There is indeed such a thing as a real if perverted pleasure in a gloomy cynicism. Thus the breaking of the snare restores to life its zest, and to me the sense of delighted wonder with which I looked at life when I was a boy and still uncorrupted. That innocence came through ignorance. This restored innocence comes through knowledge, but knowledge not only or chiefly of man but of God in his power and love. So secondly I have an overwhelming sense of delight in living and love for life; and you will realise the difference this must make to enrich the work of a physician.

The third immediate difference which becoming a follower of Jesus brings I can put more briefly. Not only does it now seem worth while to pray; it is inevitable that one does pray. I told you once, long ago, that I had always been interested in prayer, and had wanted to do it. But it seemed absurd unless and until you could believe in a God who was worth praying to. I could not, any more than you, pay that honour to the old Greek gods and goddesses, for they were all too human. Nor could I bring myself to pray to the kind of God in whom I always did believe because, in my conception of him, he was all too inhuman. But now I know at last the true God who, on the one hand, is the majestic omnipotent creator of the world, and on the other, became a man in history in Jesus. To him, once known, you can pray just as easily and naturally as you can worship.

You asked 'what does it feel like to be a Christian?', and all I have written so far is perhaps a little self-regarding. This is certainly what it feels like to me. But what of all the many others like me? It is not easy to answer for them, and even in the spiritual intimacy of life within the church, people still have their natural and right reserves. In relation to God, what I have already written about myself would in some degree be true of practically all the others, except for the Jews—or most of them. In relation to other people, what we all find is that the

word Fellowship means something new, something so rich
that we had not dreamed of it as possible, something so new
that we had never heard of it. How can I put it to you? We
Christians are members one of another; the hurt of one of us
is the hurt of all of us, and the joy of one is the joy of all. There
are for us no longer purely private joys and sorrows.

If the members of the church were all of one type, all Jews
say, or all Roman officials and their wives, there would be
nothing very remarkable in that. But they are all as different
in social and racial origin as they well could be. There are
perhaps a hundred of us, and of these most are free working
men and women, who find it hard to make enough money
to live for they are heavily handicapped in the labour market
by the slaves to whom, of course, no one need pay any wages.
The result is that in Antioch, as in Rome and every other
great commercial city, the lower class freemen and the slaves
hate each other like poison, and whenever there is a riot in
the streets the rivalry between these two social groups is
certain to be at the bottom of it. But in the church we have a
good number of slaves as well as poor freemen, and there,
and there alone no barrier divides them. We have a few
Romans. Some are government officials, some are army
officers, and some are common soldiers. But in the church
they take no notice of their ranks, and behave as though they
were equals, as indeed they are in the love of God and their
debt to him through Christ our Lord. We have some Syrian
merchants, some Greek public officials, lawyers, and teachers in
the municipal schools. There are also quite a number of Jews,
and some of these do find it hard to treat those of us born in
other nations as their equals and their friends. But many
succeed, and the president of our church here is himself a Jew
and a working coppersmith. He holds that office with the
glad consent of us all.

Tell me, do you think that anywhere else in the world, or

under the aegis of any of the old religions, it would be possible for people so racially and socially various to be so closely and regularly associated together in perfect unity one with another? You know well how tall and unscaleable the barriers are which life builds to separate freemen from slave, officer from soldier, Roman from Jew, Greek from Syrian, adult from child, man from woman. But for those who have accepted Jesus Christ as divine Lord and Saviour the barriers seem no longer to matter. Though throughout the whole range of heathen life, in which we Christians have still to bear our full part, the barriers remain, yet inside the church they have already been swept away. Here we have for the first time in the history of the world the promise of the new society of equality and brotherhood, where men and women are no longer Jews or Romans, bond or free, Greeks or barbarians, but just human beings for whom Christ died, and who love each other because they love the one true God. And I am part of it, in at the birth of it. Do you wonder that every day is a new day and that I know I shall go through it rejoicing?

ALMOST you persuade me to become a Christian; and if
there is a church in Antioch I suppose there is one in
Rome too. No doubt I could find out if I chose. But I do not
choose—not yet. For *almost* is not *quite*, and you will have to
tell me a great deal more, and answer for me many of my
disbelieving questions, before I could dream of taking such a
step myself. You know how deeply I value my uncommitted
freedom. I shall need a lot of convincing before I exchange it
for the obligations of a fixed system of belief and a new set of
habits. Yet I am indeed predisposed to think well of any religion
which can do so much to make happy my two dear, but
previously restless and frustrated friends, Luke and Silvanus. If
I ask you some questions, then, it is not, believe me, to mock,
but to learn.

What makes you think that this new religion is the only
thing in the world today which has the power to take men of
different races and bind them into a unity? I know the Stoics
can't do it, or the followers of Epicurus, but Rome can and
does. You know our formula as well as I know it myself: 'A
citizen of any of the provinces of the Roman Empire is a
citizen of Rome'. It makes no difference what colour, what
religion, what nationality a man is, he is a Roman. You are a
Greek, Silvanus a Jew, and I a Roman. No matter, we are all
Romans, I by birth, you and Silvanus by adoption. In my
office I have six clerks and six copyists. Three of the copyists
are slaves and do not count. Of the rest four come from
northern Italy, two from Sicily, two from North Africa, and
the last is from Germany. But we are all Romans, and we all

get on quite happily together. In this very office in fact Rome has taken men of very different nationalities and social backgrounds and made them (what is your phrase for it?) 'members one of another'. I do not doubt that you followers of Jesus Christ can do the same, but you must not say or even imply that no one else can do it, or even that you did it first.

I am not searching for the unity of the nations in the Roman peace for I already see it every day. What I am trying to find is something very different and I am wondering if your new religion can succeed where all the others have failed, and show me where it is. What I want and what Rome wants is not justice, not law, not peace (she has them all), but power. I do not mean authority or force. These, irresistibly, are at our command. What I mean is a moral power, the power to cure our own corruption. There we are powerless. With all our legions we are still morally impotent. The most adult and experienced of all nations, we are as helpless as babies and as corrupted as satyrs.

The nature and the name of this corruption is cruelty—and cruelty of the worst kind, deliberate and lascivious. In any state criminals have to be executed. It has been left to us to do this by the most cruel of all methods, crucifixion. Has any other nation ever instituted so disgraceful a way of making public holiday as the *Games* (note that dreadful word) of the amphitheatre? When we conquer and civilise a new province, we give it stable law, we give it peace, and then we give it its own amphitheatre, by which we waken all the worst passions of the human nature of its citizens and ensure that in their turn they become as debauched as our own rabble here, finding in the sight of blood and the infliction of death the most exquisite of their pleasures.

It has now come to this; in Rome cruelty is so nearly universal among us, that few notice it and few care to censure it. The Games have taken so deep a hold on our people that no emperor, however apparently unshakable his authority, dare interfere with them. To diminish this the most heinous of all the forms of cruelty with which we have cursed the world and ourselves would at once invite the most dangerous of revolutions. We have created a monster, and we can so little control it that we are being wholly corrupted by it, and we are helpless unless we can find some new power which at present no one can even imagine. Now, can we look for this power in your new religion? If we can, it will have the support and sympathy of all thinking and humane m~n, and your friend Theophilus among them.

But I do not know what to look for in this religion, for you tell me a little of its effect on the social life of its votaries but nothing of what it is in itself. It centres upon this man Jesus of whom you say that he is your Saviour and Lord. From what does he save? Of what is he Lord? Where is his authority? What little I know of him comes from reports of Pontius Pilate and his successor. They draw a picture of a gentle, deluded peasant whose skill in curing diseases won him a small following, with which he sought to create a national movement of religious reform. But in this he failed, grotesquely and pitifully. His trial was such a mockery of Roman justice that it still makes me angry to think of it, and his sentence savage and quite unnecessary. But that is all I know, and it leaves me very puzzled. I pity the man deeply. I believe that he was harmless and gentle and kind. I even believe that he may well have had a natural and innate skill to heal diseases. But are these really the materials of a world religion? Can such a peasant drive out all the old gods? Is there likely to reside in such as he was the power to drive out of Rome her entrenched corruption? It is clear that this is exactly what Silvanus and you think. You would both say Yes with enthusiasm to all these questions. But why? Any reasonable person would dismiss you both as credulous fools. But I know well that you are not fools and not in the least credulous, either of you. Then how comes it that you can possibly believe such things?

It may well be, of course, that my own knowledge of this Jesus and his religion is so scanty that I am asking the wrong questions. But if so, it is for you to tell me more and teach me the meaning of it. I pray that you will for I truly want to understand. I know what he did, but tell me who he was, where he came from, who his friends were, what he stood for, what he taught, and wherein his evident attraction lies.

Tell me more, too, of this church of yours at Antioch. You say that you meet there regularly to worship Jesus, and that the social and racial barriers between you have fallen down. That is good, but very vague and limited. What do you and your friends actually do when you meet? What difference does this religion make to you in your daily lives? Above all, show me in all this the power to undermine corruption itself. We never needed it more or saw it less. I want to know. I have a weakly fluttering hope and I want to reach certainty. Your friendly instruction would perhaps help.

Barnabas to James the Elder   ANTIOCH
                                                       A.D. 36

BLESSED be God, my brother and Father in the Lord, who
through your voice has bestowed on me this ministry.
For, as I will tell you in its due place in this letter, I plan to
stay here for the present, and, at their invitation, to continue
to build up and to serve the Lord's people in Antioch.

This is indeed a church which warms your heart. More than
any I have yet seen, it is an assembly of faithful men and
women in which the Lord Jesus would most delight. This is
the more remarkable in that very nearly all of them became
Christians (as we are called in Antioch) long after the Lord
was received up into Heaven, and so never saw him or heard
him or knew him in the days of his flesh. 'Blessed are they',
he said to Thomas, 'who have not seen and yet have believed',
and this blessing has been bestowed in full measure upon the
brethren with whom I have been worshipping during the last
three months. Never have I known such mutual love as these
people show to each other, and yet it cannot be easy for them
or come naturally to them, for they are of all nations and all
classes. In the world they would soon be at each other's throats.
The Greek would secretly spit at the Roman, the Syrian would
cross the road to avoid the Cypriot's shadow, and the Jew
(alas, that it is so) would despise and exploit them all. The
abyss between wealth and poverty, freedom and servitude
would never be bridged. The strong strain of vice, both natural
and unnatural, for which very ample provision is quite publicly
made here, accentuates and more deeply embitters these racial
and social divisions. In the world in Antioch, it is natural to
be vicious, and goodness is possible only by grace. But in the

church this grace is to be had for the asking, and it has been richly received, for among our Christian people we have representatives of all these types, and they do genuinely love each other and each seeks the good of the other in the blessed give-and-take of the divine love which the Lord has for them all.

This church is in some ways very like and in others unlike the church in Jerusalem. As they are gathering for worship the talk is in so many languages that it sounds like Babel. But they can all speak the Common Tongue of Greek, and the Services, done in that tongue, follow closely the pattern of the apostolic worship in Jerusalem. But let me describe for you the gathering of the church here on the first day of any week. It will be the best way of answering at least some of the questions you sent me here to ask.

The city of Antioch is joined to the pleasure gardens of the Daphne by a long, straight, wide road; and it is bordered by large white villas, each standing in its own extensive grounds. There the wealthy live. As each one vies with his neighbour to enjoy the finest garden of them all, and these gardens run down the slope from the villas to the road, all blazing with flowers and green with lawns, this must be one of the most beautiful roads in the whole of the Empire. One of the villas at the Daphne end of the road is owned by a young Roman couple, Servetus and his wife Flavia, who are Christians. Servetus inherited it from his father, a Roman official; and in the large hall of this house the church meets. There are at present about sixty members of the church, with perhaps another twenty catechumens who are preparing for baptism.

There, early on a Sunday morning, the church assembles. Both socially and racially it is a very mixed gathering indeed. The road outside is lined with chariots, coaches, and farm wagons, though most come on foot. Servetus and Flavia greet them as they enter, making most perhaps of the poorest

and of the children. They all know each other very well, and
for perhaps half an hour they stroll in the garden and talk.
Then a bell rings, and they gather in the great hall. They sing
a hymn. More often than not it is our favourite at home in
Jerusalem.

> Awake thou that sleepest and arise from the dead,
> And Christ shall give thee light.

Then the service follows its normal course. There is a reading
from the Scriptures, and an exposition of the meaning of the
passage read, and then prayers are said for the sick and suffering.
After that come the exhortations in which any of the brethren
may join as the Spirit moves him. Each may speak of the
Lord's goodness to him, and they all seek to build each other
up to a still firmer cleaving to the Lord. Another hymn
introduces the sermon or instruction, which I generally give,
and tell them what I remember of the teaching, the parables,
and the life of Jesus our Lord, for you would be surprised to
find how very little these Gentile Christians know of what he
said and did, apart from what he was and how he suffered and
rose from the dead. That, of course, they must know and
assent to before they are baptised. Now it is the time of the
Eucharist, so the catechumens leave the church, and always at
this point the hymn of their instruction

> God was manifest in the flesh,
> Justified in the spirit,
> Seen of Angels,
> Preached unto the Gentiles,
> Believed on in the world,
> Received up into glory

is sung; and as they go a collection is taken from them
and all of us, and with this money we help any who are
sick or in need. This help is not limited to the Christians.

We often give some of the money to people still in the world who are enduring some grievous affliction. Nicholas, or one of the other deacons, goes with them to give them their instruction. The doors are shut and locked, and I proceed to the breaking of the bread and blessing of the wine for the eucharist of the Lord's blessed presence with his faithful and committed people. Sometimes, however, I go and do the Eucharist for them at one of the other churches, for in Antioch we already have four of them, and as more and more of those who should be saved are added to the Lord these four will have to be increased. This is in fact one of our pressing practical problems here, and blessed be God that it is so.

In the months which I have spent here I have got to know all these dear people very well, for I have used much of my time in visiting them in their homes, and so there has been plenty of opportunity for me to get to know a good deal about each one of them. There is a Greek physician here called Luke who has been so great a help to me that without him my task would have been much harder. He is a physician of skill and eminence, though in this not unlike others of his kind. He has very great natural sympathy and creates the sense of trust wherever he goes, but even these qualities, though more rare, are mercifully not unique among physicians. But Luke's sympathies are not casual but passionate, and he has the gift of making each person he meets feel that he thinks of him as the most important person in the world. Thus people so trust him that they pour out their troubles before him, and I suppose that he is the guardian of more secrets of human lives than perhaps any other man in all Antioch. In his dealings with people God has given this Gentile the grace to be more like our dear Lord than anyone else I know, and he is as well a highly cultivated and widely travelled man in whose company it is always a particular pleasure to be.

He has recently become one of our catechumens, but long

before that he was the physician and confidant of most of the
Christians here, with whom, though he would not commit
himself at that stage, he seemed to be temperamentally in accord
and sympathy. The reason for his long hesitation was that the
Way seemed to him to be but a new form of the ancient
Jewish way; and he would have nothing to do with a religion
or way of life, however exalted, which separated people (as
Jews and Gentiles) instead of uniting them. I still do not know
just why he changed his mind and asked to be prepared for
baptism, for in spite of his power to draw confidences out of
other people, I have noticed that he maintains a firm reserve
about his own; and in all his friendliness he never loses his
dignity. To me, as you can imagine, he has been most helpful,
for he knows the people in the church here, one by one, with
an intimacy and thoroughness that no one else, not even
Nicholas the coppersmith, can approach. He has never broken
their confidences to me, but he has smoothed my path in getting
to know them sufficiently to estimate their needs, and lay them
before you.

First, then, I will tell you what seems to me the strength of
the church in Antioch; and then I will tell you its point of
weakness and danger. Its strength is not its unity, its zeal, its
devotion. It has all these things, but so have other churches
elsewhere. But it is what they are not, a largely Gentile church,
in which there are more than twice as many Gentiles as Jews.
This is what gives it its strength and character. For most
Christians here this religion, this 'Way' is totally new. Only
the Jews among them relate it to the ancient religion of the
Hebrews, or see it as a development of, and inseparable from the
religion of Moses and the Prophets. These Gentile brothers of
ours have none of the Jewish feeling for historical continuity.
This Way is for them a novelty in history, a new departure and
a new creation, and their life began on the day they found it.
Moreover, so many races are represented in the fellowship of

the church in Antioch that it is particularly rich in political experience. Thus it is always trying to piece together its instinctively wide view of the world and this new religion which, because it believes it to be The Truth and not merely one part of the truth, it believes can save the world from the betrayal of its own corruption. Our people here are always searching for a programme of Christian expansion, always looking for new fields to conquer. Because it is largely Gentile it is the most missionary of churches. For exactly the same reason it has a sense of the reality and need of this wide world of the Roman Empire which is hardly less vivid than its sense of the truth of God in heaven. Here heaven and earth are equally tethered and the Antioch Christian, enthralled and excited by the absolute novelty (as it seems to him) of what he has found, is determined to use it for the redemption of kingdoms as well as of people. He does not believe, as so many of our friends do, that the end of this world is imminent.

And of course, as you will already have seen, the very strength of this church is also its danger. It has a world and not a national point of view. It sees this Way as the Truth of all truths for all people. Redemption through Jesus our Lord is for all equally, in all places and at all times. It concedes that this blessed gift of God to the whole world came through the Jews, and is their gift. But it refuses to recognise any patent rights in it that the Jews may claim, and all the more so because the Jews did crucify the Lord, and, as a nation, have since rejected him. This is certainly how the Gentiles among us think, and they are heavily in the majority. Indeed what I have written in the last paragraphs is very nearly an exact quotation of what Luke has urged on me in many talks, and he speaks for the mind of all our Greek, Roman, and Syrian Christians here. But we also have our Jews, and it is very hard for them to think in the same way. Perhaps, except for the grace of God, it is nearly impossible when it comes to translating these principles of judgement into practical repudiations of habit and custom, as over circumcision and the obligations of obedience to the details of the Law. I who am a Christian, a Jew of the Dispersion, and a Cypriot can completely understand both points of view, and sympathise with both too. This clash, for that is what is coming, is not between good and evil but between two forms or types of good. For this reason it is dangerous, and you and our apostolic brothers in Jerusalem will need very great wisdom to deal with it.

As always, it is over practical details that the trouble comes to a head. The Cypriot in me writes the word *Details* and the Jew in me at once adds the gloss that *Details* is the wrong word since they are not trifling but important. Take the rite of circumcision. Issachar, the young and fiery leader of the Jewish section of our church, rather tactlessly suggested to Luke that as this Way is a Jewish way he ought to be circumcised before he is baptised. He was honestly astonished, I think, at the burst of rage he provoked from that most controlled and even-tempered of men. Under no circumstances, said Luke, would he submit to an operation so barbarous and degrading, nor would he have anything whatever to do with any divinity which demanded it. Then he re-collected himself and apologised for having spoken so angrily. But he would not withdraw the substance of his protest; and in this he undoubtedly spoke for the rest of the Gentiles. Of the many male Gentiles who have been baptised here and become true followers of the Way, there is not one who has accepted circumcision. To Issachar and his friends, this is a grief which is fast becoming a grievance.

But it is over the daily and weekly demands of the Law that the real clash comes. A man cannot be circumcised more than once. He can keep or refuse to keep the Sabbath every week, and can eat or refuse to eat unlawful food every single day. Here the Jews among us are in a real predicament. Because they have become Christians they have not ceased from being Jews, and it is inconceivable to them that any such demand should be made. Nor is it made, not at least in so many words. But the position of a Jew who becomes a Christian is quite different from the position of a Greek, in that it is far less demanding to be a good Greek than to be a good Jew. The Jew must still observe all his obligations of obedience to the Law of Moses, and must add to them the further obligations of membership of the church. The Greek is bound only by the obligations of a Christian. He has few or none of his own. Thus the Christian Jew must keep holy his own Sabbath day. He must worship in the synagogue, and he must refrain from recreation as well as from work. Having done that he must then keep holy the Christian first day of the week, in which he must worship in the church. In what other ways the Christian marks the sanctity of the day on which Jesus was raised from the dead have not been determined or laid down, so far as I know. But in Antioch it has come to be accepted that the Christians do as little worldly business on that day as is possible. The Gentiles expect their Jewish brothers to worship with them on the first day of the week, and the Jews gladly do this. But when the Jews expect the Gentiles to worship with them in the synagogue on the Sabbath, the Gentiles see no reason why they should, and do not.

Apart from 'keeping the Sabbath Day holy', the daily practical details and requirements of the Law are causing constant trouble and distress. A Greek Christian, let us say, invites his friends in the church to dinner, and some Jewish Christians are among the guests. By the strict letter of the Law the Jews should not accept because it is forbidden to them to eat with Gentiles. But they do accept, after a slight struggle with their consciences. Then they find that their Greek host has, in blissful ignorance of the Law, provided food which it is not right for a Jew to eat. What must they do? Refuse to eat it—and so break fellowship? Or eat it—and break the Law? It is really most difficult for them, and so this kind of clash continues in a score of different ways.

The Christians, says the Greek, are a church, not a new Jewish sect. But the Jews say they are a church *and* a Jewish sect. It is idle to expect the Greek to feel any loyalty to the Mosaic Law. But it is also idle to expect the Jew to cease to be loyal to the Law. He cannot, and perhaps he ought not, suddenly to put away from him the whole of his training from infancy and the tradition of his race. Yet the Lord's Salvation is for all, and Gentile and Jew must live in fellowship in the same church. In Antioch the Gentile is heavily in the majority. But so he soon will be everywhere else outside Judea since the Jews as a nation have rejected the Saviour, and in any case there are far more Gentiles than Jews in the world. On any calculation, therefore, it will be quite impossible to maintain the position that the Christian is bound by the Law of Moses; and though my heart aches for the dilemma in which the present generation of Jewish Christians is placed, yet I counsel that some means be found whereby the Christians are declared to be free of the obligations of the Jewish Law. We have already declared that God has granted repentance and salvation to the Gentiles as well as to the Jews, and have admitted them to the Church. Having granted the one freedom, we are bound to grant the other. The only real questions are How and When.

Meanwhile I must take what steps I can to keep the mixed church here on an even keel. I fear the fanatical, legalistic spirit of Issachar, even while I understand and sympathise with the inner torment which drives him. So I am going to Tarsus to persuade Paul to join me for a time in the apostolic charge of the growing church in Antioch, for he has had exactly the same legal training as Issachar and has faced and overcome exactly the same inner conflict. To him Issachar may listen. He will not listen to anyone else.

Luke to Theophilus   ANTIOCH
                                              A.D. 40

THE months which have passed since your letter came have been very full and busy for me, and, boon of boons, they have been completely happy. Almost I have forgotten the years of sad disillusion and despair. One is delivered from the disease first, and then, but more slowly, even from the pain, though not the memory of having suffered from it. That old life is buried deep in almost another world. This new life is here now in this world, and though it is now half a year old it is as though it began yesterday. Its joy and its thrill lose neither their strength nor their novelty.

But to describe all this to you, as you ask, is to set about analysing a mystery or dissecting a rose. Mysteries have a habit of remaining mysterious and to questions about them neat and pat answers can very seldom be given. One does not need to be a Christian to be a man of prayer. Many men and women, of any religion and of none, habitually pray, and among them, as I know, His Excellency Theophilus. No one who prays doubts that something happens as a result which would not have happened without it. The effect of the prayer is ascertainable fact. How it comes to be fact is mystery. The thing works but none can say how it works. The praying man knows this for himself, and does not try to explain the inexplicable. To himself he does not even pose it as a problem. To those who stand outside his experience and never pray he does not, if he is wise, attempt to explain, for they exclude themselves from any understanding.

So it is with your questions about the meaning and power of the new life in the church of Jesus of Nazareth. You stand outside a mystery and I, by God's grace, inside it. Come inside and taste and see. That is my prayer for you. I will try as best I can to answer your questions. But the real meaning and quality of the life to which these answers point cannot be described in words. They can only be experienced, and that from inside the community of the mystery. For me to write to you about the details of our worship would therefore be misleading. Because I cannot capture the essential mystery of the truth which lies at its heart, a description of it would seem to you trivial in its very simplicity. Indeed, as compared with all the public worship offered to any of the pagan deities or surrounding the mysteries of Apollo, our Christian worship is so simple and undramatic as to seem sparse and bare. You yourself might perhaps be present at it, and see it for the first time. If you did I think you would say to yourself, 'Is there really nothing more in it than this? It seems so completely unimpressive that I simply can't imagine why it has captured my friends Silvanus and Luke. What in the world is there to appeal to them?' And you would look round casually at the worshippers, and they would seem to you very, very ordinary, and even mediocre. But all that would be because you were looking at it critically from the outside. No one can understand what it really means to us unless he is himself part and parcel of it, standing on the inside of the circle, and sharing in the deep experience of worshipping our Lord Jesus.

Therefore I come to the question to which you seem to attach most importance: Does this Way offer the moral power needed to save the Empire from her own corruption? Yes certainly, because it offers the power of God himself mediated through Jesus our Lord who laid down his life to save the world and all the people in it, and whose choice of a way of salvation was endorsed and vindicated by God when he raised him from death to life. I have seen this power at work. I have seen habitual evil-doers forgiven by it, set free, and totally changed. I have seen hesitant cowards made into brave and resolute men. It is said that even the closest friends and followers of Jesus turned their backs on him and ran for their lives when he was arrested, but today those same men equal in courage and endurance the very bravest heroes in the history of Rome. I have seen the avaricious and covetous come to despise money and repudiate its power. I could take you to see men and women once infamously renowned for their cruel brutality, and you would judge them tirelessly kind and self-effacing, as in fact they are.

So I could continue for many pages and still not tell a tenth part of what I have seen this new power do for men and women and children in their need. There is no doubt at all of it. A new power has come into the world. A new creation holding new and undreamed of possibilities of life is here. It is to be had for the asking by all who call on the name of Jesus, through whom alone it has come. We need only believe. We need only ask. And why should not this power spreading from believer to believer through the world, as it *will*, do what you ask of it, and provide that change in human hearts and lives which in the end will cure the corruption of Rome, and empty even the amphitheatre? However long it takes, that is what it can and will do in the end, for just as it makes new lives so it will also make through them new worlds. You will see for yourself what you most desire as soon as there are enough Christians sitting in the seats of authority in Rome. May that day come soon enough for you to see it, and, if I dare say it to you, to take your own share in it.

Yet here again I must not claim too much. The new and full power of God is indeed abroad in the world but it is mostly made available through human beings who, though forgiven and saved, are still fallible mortals, always liable to fail in understanding, slip into sin, and offer to God only a part of themselves, not the whole for him to use. The light is kindled but men and women have to reflect it, and the bright surfaces

they offer to the light are never completely impeccable. The
full intensity of its effulgence is shining and yet it is only seen
in part. The new power therefore is not absolute, not invariable,
not automatic. As men halt and waver in their dedication, so
that power must move on lame feet and take long to achieve
love's aims. But one by one in the end they will all be achieved,
your aim of the destruction of the amphitheatre and mine of the
abolition of poverty. The power to do these things is here. It is
in Christ. I see it every day. And there is no other comparable
power in sight or on offer anywhere in the world.

But it takes time and does not simultaneously occupy every
field of life. I must be completely honest with you, my friend,
and qualify at least one too sweeping claim which I made in
a previous letter. I wrote that within the church of Jesus Christ
all the social and racial barriers which the world has built come
toppling down. I have had to learn from experience that this is
not yet completely true. There is still a tall barrier between
Jew and non-Jew, even in the church and among Christians.
It does not divide every Christian Gentile from every Christian
Jew. The relationships between the Gentile Luke and the
Jewish Barnabas are as close and intimate and free as anyone
could wish. But there are some Jews among us who are determined to do all they can to insist that before a Greek or Roman
can become a Christian he must first become a Jew, outwardly
marked by the scar of a simple but barbarous physical operation,
and inwardly separated from other men by his obedience to all
the multitudinous requirements of the Jewish Law. Such a
demand is fantastic and absurd, but it is constantly urged by a
small and yet vigorous minority among our Jewish Christians.
So far they have had no success here in Antioch, nor, so far as I
know, in any other church. But they are pertinacious in their
arguments and resourceful in their tactics. Nor are they
particularly scrupulous. I fear them a little because what they
appeal to lies very deep in the Jewish character, and it is still in

Jerusalem, the very heart of Jewry, that the rulers of the whole of the churches of our Lord live, and the only court of appeal is composed of the fine men who were chosen friends of Jesus, but who are, nevertheless, Jews themselves, and so are bound by their ancient traditions to be sensitive to the strings our malcontents may try to pluck.

All this, however, is no more than to say that life in the church is not yet quite perfect. But it is incomparably better, richer, and fuller than life in any other religious or social circle in the world. And as though for such a moment and to meet such a danger as this God has provided us and himself with a new and unexpected weapon in the shape of a famous and rigidly orthodox young Jew, who has turned his life right round, and become a Christian, after having given all his exceptional energies to the bitter persecution of every Christian on whom he could lay hands.

His name is Paul, and he is quite the most remarkable man I have ever met in the whole course of my life. His history would not perhaps interest you very deeply, but the man whom this history has made you would find a fascinating character study. He comes from Tarsus and thus is technically a Roman citizen, but he spent most of his early life in Jerusalem and became a very brilliant student in what seems to have been the most savagely unyielding of all the religious Schools of Law in that tempestuous city. This brought him into the ranks of the Pharisees, the political-cum-religious 'party', whom Jesus was always denouncing, and by whose intrigues his crucifixion was engineered. Paul himself happened not to be in Jerusalem at that time, and so was not a party to the shameful act. But he certainly would have been for he is a particularly vehement and passionate man, and the activity of Jesus was challenging every ideal he had been trained to maintain. Thus when he returned after the Lord had risen, and found that that new Way of life had not only risen with him but was spreading fast, he threw all his tremendous energies into stamping it out. He became a ruthless inquisitor and a merciless persecutor of those early Christians. He smelled them out, harried them, brought them to judgement, and pleaded for their condemnation. Not a few of those first martyrs owed their death sentence to him. That they, being Jews, should seem to challenge the Jewish Law, which, whatever we Gentiles may think of it, had been for centuries bone of their bone and flesh of their flesh, was something he could not bear. To him it was the most heinous and unnatural of treasons, and those who, as he might have put it, flouted the whole history of their race, were not fit to live. So he gave all his single-minded enthusiasm to seeing to it that they did not live. The damage he did was enormous, and for several years no name was more feared and dreaded among Jewish Christians than Saul of Tarsus.

He sounds, you will be saying, exactly the kind of man whom I should most detest. Yes, but he was a man, not a jellyfish. He had a mind and he knew it. His eye was bright with purpose. And now, mark the sequel. This consuming purpose of his egged him on to look for fresh fields to cleanse of the detested Christians. In Jerusalem it was too easy, for there he could count on the backing of almost all socially important public opinion. He wanted to fight the Way where no one had fought it before. So he arranged to be sent to extirpate it in Damascus. There he might find his work more difficult, since he is a man who rather despises a too easy victory, and is quickly sated by it. Besides, Damascus would be a field of work of his own tilling. So he set out to travel there, when, suddenly and without any warning a mysterious event swept down upon him. He had the irresistible, inexorable vision of God, who, in the form of Jesus and speaking in his own voice, claimed him for his service. This vision was heralded by a light so bright and dazzling that Paul was temporarily blinded, and had to be led by the hand for the rest of the way. There a Christian gave

him back his sight; and, characteristically, the very first thing
Paul did was to summon all the Jewish leaders to the Damascus
synagogue. It must have been a dramatic moment, when he,
the famous scourge of all the Christians, suddenly dumbfounded
his hearers by announcing his conversion, and then began to
prove that this Jesus whose very name had been anathema to
him, was in fact not only the promised Messiah of their nation,
but actually God himself, revealed in a man. To the Paul of a
week ago no blasphemy could be more unforgivable, for
it is a first principle of orthodox Judaism that the Divine may
have no image. In the Temple, the Holy of Holies is empty.
You can imagine their astonishment and their fury. Paul barely
escaped from Damascus with his life, and he owed it to the
Christians there who contrived to get him out of the city
secretly after dark.

He went from there to live for a time as a hermit in the
loneliest parts of Arabia to give himself time to think his life
afresh. Then, when he knew what he must do, he made his
way to Jerusalem to sit for a time at the feet of those who had
known Jesus in the flesh, to learn from them all they could
tell him, and to receive their recognition of him as an accredited
Christian apostle. From there he went to Tarsus to wait his call
to service. It was my friend Barnabas who conceived the idea
of bringing him to Antioch to take charge of the church here,
and he has now been with us for several months.

What is there in all this, do you ask, which so deeply excites
my admiration? It is not his meteoric career. Certainly it has
been dramatic, but hardly unique. So sudden and complete a
change of mind and purpose is not an unknown event, and
those to whom it happens generally do deny with vehemence
what they have previously given their whole lives to assert.
It is not his outward appearance, which is frankly not impressive. Picture a little man with a twitch in his cheek and a
squeaky voice with a stammer who, if analysed in cold blood

feature by feature from crown to toe, seems to be without any particular physical distinction. He is rather short in height, with a balding head, bushy eyebrows which join above the bridge of a crooked nose that is long and winged with large, flaring nostrils. Most unattractive, you say, the very quintessence of indistinction! Yes—until you see his eyes, but they are quite wonderful, and make his outwardly contemptible bodily form a vehicle of the utmost grace and charm. He is not at all at his ease in all manners of conversation, for either he will stand moodily silent or else, when roused, he will dominate the talk and speak energetically in a rushing torrent of words, and neither his stammer nor any interruption seems to halt him.

It seems almost as though I am describing a man whom I might admire but could not possibly like. Yet I do—immensely. I like him as completely as I respect him. I can be in his company with the same degree of pleasure that I can sit at his feet. He is as interesting as he is impressive, as loving as he is formidable. But then I have looked into his eyes and felt his fire. And yet I fear that this may seem to you very pallid and unconvincing, rather like a poor picture of a great man drawn by an admiring but mediocre artist. Other letters of mine which, if you can bear them, I will write from time to time, will, I expect, fill out the details of this pen-portrait, for I know somehow that, after Jesus himself, this Christian Jew Paul is to be the biggest influence in all my life. I tell you, Theophilus, as a matter of sober considered judgement, Paul of Tarsus is likely to make more difference to the history of the world than any other living man.

But for the moment I shall be perfectly content if he can change the immediate history of the Christian church in Antioch. He has impassioned arguments with our Jewish malcontents who are so determined to make men like me into obedient Jews before they will admit that we can become free

Christians. He knows their minds and their speech from the inside and he is more a master of their subtleties than dear Barnabas could ever have been. Moreover, he occasionally loses his temper with them, which Barnabas could never have done. Most of them he has now persuaded to take and rejoice in the freedom Jesus offers them. But there remains a little knot of the obdurate, once Pharisees as he was, and still Pharisees in their own claims as he is not. Of them, I am frankly a little afraid. That is, I am afraid of what they may do—not of what they are, for in their hearts the mere thought of freedom really terrifies them. They repudiate it for themselves, and are determined to destroy it for the rest of us. We shall see what happens. So far Paul has made no impression upon them, and to them, he is still a renegade and a traitor, bent on destroying the Judaism which was once almost all the world to him, and still is to them.

Issachar to Eleazor

IN this letter one Christian Jew greets another, one old
student of the great Law School of Hillel greets another,
and one proud Pharisee greets another. But the greetings are
a cry for help, for in Antioch the Gentiles in our Christian
church, numerically far stronger than we Jews, seem bent on
driving us into becoming traitors and renegades. The Gentiles
perhaps do this in ignorance. Coming from races which never
knew the Law, they cannot understand the depth of loyalty
which the mere name of Moses inspires in men like you and me.
Yet even they, one would think, knowing that Jesus was a
Jew, should find no difficulty in accepting the logical common
sense of the idea that as he was trained by Judaism, so must
they accept its obligations if they are to be his followers. But
it is the last thing they ever think of doing. When we point
out to them the falseness of their position, they become
furiously angry, and sometimes they break out into the tirades of
abuse of all things Jewish which used to be the brand of Cain
of the accursed Samaritans. There is hardly one of them who
has accepted circumcision, who makes any attempt to keep the
Sabbath holy, who puts the least restraint on himself in what he
eats at meals. They have not consciously rejected the Law,
for it never once occurs to them that the Law can or ought to
have the least claim on them. They come to our worship of
our Jewish Messiah. By their numbers they dominate it. They
shout sickeningly about their freedom, and they think they can
be prophets and saints by the simple process of ignoring all
the rules the keeping of which can alone make people holy to
the Lord. I tell you, Eleazor, that the Christians here honestly

think of our Christian religion as a sweeping away into the forgotten darkness of the archaic the whole majestic apparatus of Moses, and his Law and ours.

Most of the Jews among us, including, alas, Barnabas, the delegate of the Apostles in Jerusalem, have come to swim contentedly in their stream. They make no attempt to bring these Gentiles to their senses. They give neither support nor help to the few of us who do try. So we avail nothing. But I am not content to avail nothing, and do not propose to be regarded here as a mere cypher.

The situation is really much worse than this, for now we have that man Paul of Tarsus. We all know his record as a persecutor of Christians. It was the first of his defiances of the Law. But that defiance one might charitably ascribe to ignorance of its inner meaning, though it is difficult to believe it of him. Eventually the Law leads him where it led you and me, into the discipleship of Jesus our Lord. But then, if you please, instead of upholding it, as he should, and using his great authority to win for it the loyalty of the Christian Gentiles, he seizes every chance he gets of arguing against it, repudiating it, proclaiming its supposed uselessness and futility, and pouring public scorn upon it for the benefit of the applauding and grinning Gentiles. He is the true renegade and traitor, for unlike the simple Barnabas and Nicholas, he knows exactly what he is doing. He actually says that Jesus came in order to set people free of the Law, and claims that the Law breakers have divine authority behind them.

I have argued, appealed, persuaded. It is all useless. I have asked the Lord's brother James to intervene and he will not. Well, he and the other apostles may choose to risk apostasy to gain a quiet life. But I will not. Nor, I believe, will you. We must force the Apostles' hands by direct action, and I have a suggestion to make to you. It is that you and I form a secret society among the Pharisee-Christians who think as we do—

and there are plenty of them. This society would have two objects. The first is to follow Paul from place to place, getting to each one soon after he has gone on to the next, and doing all that lies in our power to undo the damage he will certainly cause. I happen to know that he is soon to leave here for a missionary tour. The second is to work upon the Apostles through the pressure of the Christian Jews, and to force them into a position where they can no longer escape from declaring publicly that the full requirements of the Law of Moses are binding upon all the followers of Jesus, the Gentile equally with the Jew. I fancy that Peter is the weak link in their chain. It would not be difficult to work upon him. The details of the campaign I have in mind must wait until we can meet. So I ask you to come to see me in Antioch as soon as you can. Come secretly. We are upon secret work. It must be so. If we will the end, the saving of the Law, we must not be afraid to will the means, even if the means are backstairs intrigue.

Luke to Silvanus   ANTIOCH
                                                                A.D. 44

HAS Paul told you? I am so ignorant a beginner that I do not know how these things are done. But I suppose that just as all physicians are bound to keep careful written records of the patients they treat, so when a convert is baptised and admitted to Communion in the church, his name must appear on some list which goes to the elder brethren of the church in Jerusalem. If so, you will by now have seen it.

But it may not be done like that at all. There may even be no such thing in the world as a list of the Christians. One of the pleasant, refreshing things about the church which I have noticed is a certain happy-go-luckiness in its organisation. It gathers into its arms 'such as should be saved', to use a phrase of Barnabas's, and then it leaves them almost completely unorganised. This cheerful untidiness, so foreign to the civil service mentality of the Empire, delights me. It is one of the joys of our Freedom, and may the day never come when we Christians choke ourselves by our own forms and order, and imprison ourselves in our own jargon.

Well, whether Paul has yet told you or not, you will see that I instinctively write *We* rather than *They* and *Ourselves* rather than *Themselves*, and you will already have guessed what I write to tell you. It is that on the Lord's Day a week ago, Paul baptised me in the waters of Daphne, gave me Holy Spirit (somehow, I *know* it to be true), admitted me to the church, and sealed it by inviting me to partake along with all the others of the symbols of the body and blood of our Lord, and the actuality of his presence whenever I receive what his first friends received from his own hands on the night of his betrayal.

Three others were received and baptised with me—Persis the Letter Writer, Demeter the cattle breeder, Hassan the Syrian, who is the chief of his slaves.

Our little band of self-tormented malcontents, Issachar's Jewish faction, did what they could to spoil it all at the last moment. They asked Paul publicly and as the baptism was beginning, by what authority he, a Pharisee, made Gentiles heirs of the 'promises of Israel' without making them Israelites by the sign of circumcision. You can imagine how Paul dealt with them. With the greatest difficulty he kept his temper, but he silenced them all the more effectively for that. Personally I am very sorry for them. Their conflict may be of their own making, but it tears them in two, and it must be horribly painful. But I also fear them. In the long run they cannot win, but in the short run they may do us all great damage.

This small awkwardness, however, is but a single drop in the ocean of my joy. I feel as Ulysses did when after all his wanderings he at last stepped ashore on to the beloved land of Ithaca. He had come home and so have I. I could not, even to you, describe and expose all my deepest feelings. I cannot play the part of the quivering ecstatic, and it would not be seemly if I could. Nor would that mantle fit me, for it really seems to me as though a new and overwhelming principle has come into my life to order it and make a coherent, single pattern of its scattered parts. This principle is personal. It is in fact a person, Jesus Christ our Lord, who has saved me and saves me afresh every day that passes, and will at my last end receive my soul into the quickening of eternal life. Everything that by native inheritance I was to begin with, and everything which has come to me in my life seems now to be held together and intensified by Christ my Lord to whom I give thanks. Life is not senseless, as once it was, and human endeavour is no longer a futility. My life began all over again a week ago, and I find it wonderful.

To anyone but you, all that would seem the raving of the quivering ecstatic—'speaking intemperately with tongues', Paul would call it. But it is of the problem it sets me that I really want to consult you. To what purpose is this joy? By the mercy of God I have been called into it—but for what? Simply in order to be a better physician than I once was? God knows that is a worthy aim. Did not our Lord declare war on all disease? Yet I cannot think that this is his whole end and purpose for me. All my days and in all circumstances I continue to be a physician, and to put what skill I have at the free disposal of all who suffer. The oath of the Christian does not cancel the oath of Hippocrates; it underlines it. But I cannot escape from the conviction that God may have some special work for me to do, which must be added to my ordinary work as a physician. I am quite sure about this, and my only question is what this new work is to be.

I have some gleams of light about this which I want to put before you. As you probably know, John Mark has recently been visiting us here, and when he spoke to us in church he told us all that he remembered about what happened to Jesus on that dreadful night in the Garden of Gethsemane. He was there himself, it seems, and only just escaped from being arrested. It was a moving story, as naturally it must be, but what astonished me was how little of it I had heard before. I knew, of course, of the Last Supper, that afterwards the disciples went with the Lord into the garden, that the traitor Judas betrayed him by kissing him again and again. I knew too that there were two trials, before Caiaphas and before Pilate, and that he was crucified, and that God raised him from the dead. But beyond this I knew almost no detail at all. I had never heard about the disciples falling asleep twice when they had been told to watch and pray. Nor did I know anything of how he bore himself on the cross, or of what he said. What was even more surprising was to discover that Paul seemed to know not much more than I did, while most of the other followers of the Way here knew even less.

Afterwards I took John Mark home with me and we talked for hours. I wanted him to tell me more of the Lord's life in Palestine than there had been time for him to tell us all in church. I wanted to know much more about his miracles of healing, and to hear about his teaching, and how he dealt with his friends and his enemies, and all the people he encountered who were neither friendly nor hostile. I have always wanted to know so much more detail about these things than my elder brothers in the Faith have ever told me. But it was all rather disappointing. Mark simply did not know anything more than a few odd scraps of detail here and there. What passed before his eyes in the Garden he knew exactly. But what happened before that, of the links in the chain of cause and event which led Jesus ever to be in the Garden, and created the implacable hostility which caused him to be arrested and put on trial for his life, Mark could throw so little light that it almost seemed as though the sufferings of Jesus were uncaused. It made the story of his betrayal and his death appear to be what in fact it could not have been, ugly and black and unrelieved by even the slightest gleams of hope. I think this was because as Mark told it, it made so formless a story, a climax suspended in mid-air, unprepared and unresolved.

Now all the knowledge which Mark appeared not to have is still there to be found, but it needs to be gathered and then put together in a coherent pattern. You yourself must know a good deal of it, and Peter and John probably have more knowledge still. Out of all the twelve Apostles only two are dead. The memories of the other ten can still be gathered and preserved if someone will make it his business to do this. Then Judea and Samaria must still be crowded with people who met the Lord and spoke with him. Some of those whom he healed must still be alive to tell their story. But soon most of those who had the huge privilege to know him in the flesh will grow old, and then one by one they will die. If the knowledge of the events of his mission is to be preserved for the Christians who come after us someone must at once begin to gather and record it. And if the religion of Jesus is to be the religion of the whole world, and his church is to be spread into every corner of the globe and sing her way down all the ages of time, then it seems to me essential that every scrap of knowledge of his life among us should be carefully collected and preserved. Our whole Faith is faith in him, and we must do what we can to be sure that our descendants know in whom we have believed.

Without a written record this will be impossible. We cannot rely on the memories and the word of mouth traditions. As they grow old the memories even of the saints become inaccurate and distorted. Some events they hold vividly as long as life lasts, but others, not less important, they forget. Moreover, stories which pass from mouth to mouth always get distorted and after a time they tend to have little resemblance to what actually happened. Six people may observe the same event. But ask those six separately about it a week later and already you will have six quite different accounts of it which do not tally in detail. It is not enough to rely on a tradition. If you do what you get is legend and not history. Nor is it enough simply to transcribe even the first-hand accounts of those who were themselves eye-witnesses. They have to be critically sifted, and then the whole material has to be worked into a coherent story having pattern and shape. The good news of what God has done through Jesus our Lord must be artistic history, and he who attempts such a task must be equally historian and artist, having the characteristic consciences of both.

Tell me the truth. Do you think that I have these qualities, for I feel more and more drawn to attempt the task? Do I delude myself in supposing that this is what God wants me to do? It was Theophilus who first put this into my mind when he asked me to tell him more about the life of Jesus *before* he was crucified. I could not do it because I did not know enough of it, and cannot find that the Christians I meet every day know it either. Before I can give Theophilus his answer I shall have to write a book, and before I can write a book I must gather and sift the facts. It will take some years, and I hope you think they would be rightly spent.

LETTER FIFTEEN

Issachar to Eleazor

NOW is our chance! Come, and come at once. Wait no longer than to read this letter. Then gather all the brethren of the League for the Defence of the Law in Jerusalem, and bring them with you. They are bound by their oath to obey the summons. But it is imperative that there be no delay whatever. If we wait, the opportunity which the Lord has suddenly given us will vanish, and I count on your arrival and theirs here within seven days.

Paul the renegade and Barnabas his weak tool have delivered themselves into our hands. They, together with John Mark, have suddenly sailed away to Cyprus to found the church there. It is their own version of a lawless church. Naturally, it would be. The only kind of church they care about is as much Gentile and as little Jewish as possible, in which the name of Moses will never be so much as spoken, and his Law will never even be heard of. To that, or nearly to that, they have reduced the church here. But they have gone, leaving only Nicholas to take their place, and he will not be able to prevail against us. There is a vacuum and we will fill it, and force the church back to its true and only foundation, the Law of Moses, accepted and refounded by Jesus.

It has all happened quite suddenly. Paul and Barnabas think the church in Antioch has sent them to preach the Gospel to the Gentiles of Cyprus. The church thinks so too. All its members are full of references to the Holy Ghost. You might think that they had tamed him by their talk and had him in their pockets. They have no idea at all that I, Issachar, might have had something to do with it. Paul has so deep a hold on the

people here that only in his absence can his work be undone. So
it was necessary to procure that absence. Holy Ghost indeed! He
might have caused their ecstasies, but it was I who used them.

I wish you had been there, for it was a very pretty scene. The
church was gathered for its worship, and this worship followed
its customary pattern. First, Barnabas expounded the story of
Abraham and Isaac as pre-figuring the Lord's death. Then there
was a hymn, and Nicholas said some prayers. Then Paul rose
to his feet and delivered one of his interminable moral exhortations. A second hymn followed, and then anyone else who had
a message to give was invited to give it. Two men then fairly
leaped to their feet. One is a Greek and the other Syrian, both
of them so simple-minded as to be almost mentally deficient.
They quaked, they shook, they quivered like a jelly. Their
eyes rolled and their mouths frothed. Luke watched them with
distaste written all over his elegant face, Paul with anxiety.
But he who talks so incessantly about freedom could hardly
bid them be silent. Then, after some writhings in torment, their
mouths opened, and sounds came forth. They were unintelligible noises, quite meaningless. Isaiah called this sort of
thing 'Chirping and muttering', and he, you will remember,
spoke of it with unsparing condemnation. But then, to these
Gentile Christians, taught by Paul, Isaiah is nothing and less
than nothing.

Now Paul has a theory that when such ignorant people
'speak with tongues', as he always calls it, there must be an
interpreter to translate. So it occurred to me that this time I
might be the interpreter. I claimed the privilege before anyone
could forestall me,

'Our brothers have been visited by the Holy Ghost', I said,
very slowly and impressively. 'And through them he bids us
separate Paul and Barnabas for a time to go to preach the Gospel
in Cyprus and Pamphylia. They are to go swiftly as the ambas-
sadors of the church in Antioch'.

It worked. The two ecstatics nodded their heads, and the whole assembly was immediately charmed by the idea. 'Yes', they shouted, 'That is what must be done'. One or two promptly claimed that the same thought had been given to them some weeks earlier in their private prayers. We then went on to the Eucharist, and after that Paul and Barnabas formally accepted the charge. They had been left no way of escape.

So now they are gone, and the field is clear. Bring all members of the L.D.L. We shall then have enough to prevail, and I know what we will do. I will not write it now but tell you when you come. Just as Israel was saved by a purged remnant, so must the church here be purged of those who will not accept the Law as binding them. A remnant will be left, but however small it will be Law-abiding, and on it we can build anew. That is our task and I think we shall be equal to it, and my plans prevail.

LETTER SIXTEEN

Nicholas to Silvanus   ANTIOCH
                                                         A.D. 47
(Written by the hand of our brother Persis,
Public Scribe of Antioch.)

HONOURED Sir, something terrible has happened and I verily believe that the devil has got into our church here just as the Lord Jesus said he would, but that was to be a sign of the near end of the world, and I do not think it is ending, but often lately I've wished it would and quickly too. Truly, sir, I would rather have died than see our dear brethren fighting and quarrelling and abusing each other as they are doing now. To think that we should have come to such a pass and so soon after dear Barnabas and Paul have gone away on the Lord's work, and now dear Luke, looking as if he had been suddenly kicked in the face by a favourite horse, has gone away to Troas and says, sir, he isn't never coming back. And no one knows what's happened to Paul and Barnabas, perhaps they're dead for all I know, and they left me in charge and what they are going to say to me when they do come back I really don't know. I ought to have stopped all this, I know I ought, but how could I? Can you come, sir, and put it all right again? At least will you tell me so that I can tell them that our elder brother James hasn't said what they say he has? I don't for a second believe that that dear, kind old man could possibly have said such things, but Issachar and the others swear he did, and there are so many who believe him and not me. Now if I could have a letter from James to read out—but I hardly like to bother a man as important and busy as he is, and I thought perhaps that you, sir, wouldn't mind doing it for me, seeing as you live so near him.

Persis says I must get my breath and start again. He can't keep up with me, and you won't have any idea what it's all about. I'm sorry to be so muddled, sir, but, oh dear, I am so upset!

Well, sir, it's like this. For a little time after we had sent Paul and Barnabas and Mark away to Cyprus the life of our church went on much as usual. We worshipped and prayed as we always do, particularly of course for our three brothers in foreign parts, and we even had a few new converts whom I baptised. Then Issachar said that some of the Christian Pharisees from Jerusalem were coming to visit us, so we all got ready to welcome them, and they came and were very nice to us for a bit, and we were pleased to see them. I suppose, perhaps, that Eve was pleased at first to see the serpent, and thought it made her life a bit more interesting like. Well, they were serpents all right, and nasty ones too.

But we didn't see that just at first. The trouble began to come when Issachar said he had a message from James, to read to us, and he said, James that is, that all Gentile Christians had got to be circumcised and keep the Law and go to synagogue on Saturdays as well as church on Sundays and not eat pork and I don't know what else, or they couldn't be Christians at all.

There was a terrible silence, and then Luke got up and said he didn't believe it, and he'd be damned if he did, and Issachar said he'd be damned if he didn't, and all his Jerusalem friends said yes that was it. They all talked and talked and they were much too clever for us and there was quite a lot of our people who took their side. Particularly when they said that James had said so and after all James was the brother of the Lord and ought to know better than anybody.

By this time our worship, our worship of the Lord Jesus God forgive us all, had turned into an uproar. Oh, it was horrible, *terrible!* Some of the brothers were shouting insults. Some were beginning to brawl, and hit out. Some others were silent, white-faced, and trembling. Issachar stood there quite still, watching with that horrid sarcastic little smile of his, and his fine Jerusalem friends went from group to group, stirring them up into a frenzy. I tried to get them all to listen to reason, and appealed to them to think what they were doing. But it wasn't any good, any good at all. In a few minutes the work of years had been undone. We'd learned to love each other, all of us, and now, in a flash, we were split into parties, hating one another at the tops of our voices. The church was disgraced, and I who was in charge of it was about as much as use a helpless baby. Sir, can we ever live it down?

'But the most horrible thing of all was still to come. After a long time the shouting stopped quite suddenly, and there was a moment of silence, and we all looked at each other, like as if we'd suddenly come to our senses and were ashamed and astonished too. Then Luke got up, white as a sheet he was, and very slowly he began to speak. 'I became a Christian of my own free choice', he said, 'and a Christian I stay. But I will no longer serve my Master among you. You, it seems, choose the Jewish Law. You will serve Moses, not Christ. You accept slavery as Paul feared. But I am a free man, a Greek not a Jew. If it is true that James, the Lord's brother and the chief among us, has really ordered this thing, then he has denied his brother and his master as Peter once did. *If* it is true. I don't believe it, but I can't disprove it. But I will not worship with you any more, nor eat bread with you, nor share the holy mysteries with you. I go from among you to serve my Lord as a hermit, as many better Christians than I have done before. I am leaving Antioch, and I am leaving it now. May God forgive you all for the evil you have done today.'

He turned his back on the church and was walking out of the room when I made a last try to stop him. But it was no good at all. He stopped a minute and said quietly to me, 'Not you, old friend. You did what you could. We shall meet and pray together again, you and I. Somehow I know it. But Antioch I leave now and for ever. A church which follows Issachar and rejects Paul is no place for me. I go to Troas, to be alone, and to think. Tell Paul when he comes back. And remember this— for the present Issachar and his friends may have prevailed, but the long future is not with them, nor with their Law, nor with their Moses. The long future is given to the true sons of Jesus, and will be bright with their glorious liberty. Let me go now, Nicholas. I still serve Jesus, my Lord and yours, but in some new way. This chapter of my life is ended. God bless and keep you and all in your house'. With that he walked out into the night and the door closed behind him. He must have started his journey to Troas at once, for I've not seen him since.

Everybody loved Luke, and they all looked shaken and appalled to hear him speak so. It might have been possible to rally them then, but I'm so slow of speech. Before I had collected myself Issachar was ready and had leaped in. 'He seems to think Antioch is another Sodom', he said, 'and he wipes the dust off his Gentile feet as a testimony against the true Christians who are faithful, as Jesus was, to the Law. Let him go. He is the beginning of the purge that will have to come before our church can be purified to serve our Master. I declare this assembly closed'. With that his friends fairly ran every-body out of the room, including me, their deacon. Since then more than half our Gentiles have turned back and walk no more with us. Some of them I saw only yesterday entering the Temple of Apollo. Just think of it! Some of the others have given in and been circumcised. We are a broken body now, and I am not fit to be a deacon, for I can do nothing to bind us together again.

Oh sir, come to our help, and assure us that our brother James has not said this wicked thing.

Theophilus to Luke ROME
A.D. 48

NO, I will not write, I told you so, even though in your letter you invite it. 'There! Now say, I told you so'. You remember writing that? Bitter words! Yet they are forgiven, if forgiveness they need. But for me to use them would be inexcusable as well as futile. I do not wish to impoverish my life by losing your friendship. In fact I did not think anything like this would happen, and therefore did not prophesy it. Nor had I taken the full measure of the Pharisees' fanatacism. One would think that a Roman colonial official had good cause to know the worst about the most obstinate and ungovernable of all sects. But no! They are too subtle, too tenacious, too deeply plunged in their self-tormenting hate for a comparatively simple-minded Roman to understand them. The fact is, I suppose, that our fundamental values are too opposed for comprehension to be possible. We Romans care most for civilisation. The Jews scorn and repudiate this civilisation, holding our noblest traditions in contempt.

Given their history, I suppose that the damage they have done to you and your Christian friends is understandable. But would to God the brunt of it had not fallen on you. If you like I will have Issachar and his friends arrested, brought to Rome, and put behind bars where they can do no more harm. You have only to say the word. It would be perfectly easy. But I do not think you will say it. You will think it an expedient which settles nothing, and you are right.

I am sorry beyond words that this has happened, but I pay you the compliment of not offering sympathy, still less pity. If I were a Christian (I am not—yet; but I am interested and curious, and from my heart I wish this religion well) I should consider that all this trouble would be likely to fall out for the good both of the individual sufferer (yourself) and of the church of Jesus. What has happened would bitterly hurt my human flesh and blood, but I trust I am philosopher enough to look beyond that, and if I did I think I should see that this evil episode would be bound to create a greater good than would have been possible without it.

Consider first your own personal position. You leave Antioch to go to Troas to make a kind of hermit of yourself. It is only what your so greatly admired friend Paul did when, in similar circumstances, he was forced to leave Damascus. His time of solitariness in the desert of Arabia was probably necessary for him. He had time to think and pray. So now have you. Moreover, Troas is not Arabia, and you are no Pharisee cum tent-maker. Troas is a port, a small one no doubt, but not uninhabited, and you are a very skilled physician. Do you really think that your solitariness will be absolute? Of course it won't. Within three days of your first arrival, I don't doubt, you were already practising your healing skill. Within a month you probably had quite a long list of patients.

How are you going to use what peace and quiet your patients leave you? It is for you to say, but you must use it and not drift aimlessly through it. In your place I should look at the large maps framed in the longest possible vistas of time. If this Christian religion is true at all it is true absolutely, not relatively. It is, if true, THE TRUTH. As such, it is bound to spread from land to land till it has enveloped the globe, and it will travel onwards in time through all the generations of humanity till the world itself at last ends. But humanly speaking, and under God, its driving power is the Gentile, not the Jew. There are so many more Gentiles in the world, and in any case (I write here as a Roman official and with his special knowledge), Judea is on the very edge of armed insurrection against Rome, and the only result will be the destruction of Jerusalem. The arm of such as Issachar is much shorter than it seems. Their power for mischief is for a moment only. Even for this moment it is a limited power. What will happen to the successes of Issachar when Paul gets back to Antioch, if Paul is the great man you believe? In a matter of weeks Issachar will be in some other wilderness and the damage he has done will be repaired.

If your church is to set out on this world-wide, world-long journey, it must put aside its Judaic swaddling clothes, or they will soon strangle it. It must travel west, jump the seas and establish itself in Europe, and then follow the western roads. They all lead to Rome. There is no future in despising spiritual statesmanship, and this should lead you all to make Rome your goal and its corruption your target. Once win Rome, and you win the whole Roman world with it. Do you not see that the very success of Issachar and all his kind forces you to look beyond Asia Minor to that great city which is the whole world's centre of gravity, and where every decision of any importance to history is taken. Issachar is not the least of the Christian's benefactors. He is forcing you to turn your back on your earlier parochialism, and to come out of the backwater of your early and perhaps too easy successes to face the centres of power in the real world.

It will be a hostile world. Make no mistake about that. I know Rome and I know her Emperor. The whole mighty power of Rome will be concentrated to destroy you, for the one thing Rome cannot tolerate is a religion claiming to be exclusively and uniquely THE TRUTH, for such a religion must set its deity above the Emperor himself, and hold the imperial authority as subordinate to its own. I foresee much suffering for you all. I foresee it for myself also, since at this moment I suppose I am writing what would seem here to be an invitation to treason. But amphitheatres and the corruption they stand for are not destroyed without the price of blood. The price will have to be paid, but without it Jesus cannot win Rome, and if he loses Rome and wins the whole world else. his mission fails.

I do not mean that you must also turn your back on your Jewish founder. If you are right in claiming that this Jesus is the creative Majesty of the universe in a human life, then plainly you take him with you wherever you go. On these terms, huge and staggering as they are, he is your religion, and it must be him, not just another way of life, that you offer. It is this astonishing uniqueness of what you Christians are offering which makes me think you may be right, and pre-disposes a cautious old philosopher like me towards belief and faith. The claim is that the God of the world let himself be murdered by a band of fanatical Jews, with our Roman governor (alas!) aiding them. I find it impossible to believe that anyone could invent so fantastic a tale. In fact, no religion has ever made claims such as this. They are so extraordinary that they appeal strongly to me, for no ordinary means of salvation are going to affect such a world as we now live in. God knows it needs to be saved, and it cannot save itself. So Jesus is no more Jewish than he is Greek or Roman. He is simply deified humanity. But somehow or other you have to register this claim, and urge it upon Greeks and Romans first, and eventually upon men and women of every unimaginable race which may in time come to inhabit the world.

You cannot hope to do this unless and until you can tell a plain and intelligible tale of Jesus' life, and this, it seems to me you cannot at present do. More than once I have asked you to tell me more about his life before he was crucified, and this you have never done. Is it because you do not know yourself? All I have gathered about him is that he was a peasant who led a religious reforming movement, that he was wrongfully and illegally arrested, condemned, and crucified, and that a few days afterwards he mysteriously came back to life again. I know nothing of what his reforming movement was like, what programme he urged, what he taught, how he won his following. He was God-made-man, you say—but what kind of a man? And if indeed God, what were the circumstances of his birth, and how was he trained as a boy, and when and how did he come to know his incredible destiny? You offer to the world a Gospel based upon a fantastic, illogical, and seemingly impossible assumption of his divinity. It may be so. I don't deny it. But you must see that you cannot hang this fantasy in a void. If anyone is to believe it, you must clothe it in a straightforward and clear account of the whole of the rest of his life. As I see it, you are basing your whole hope on the power of this Jesus to attract to himself the deepest loyalties of all sorts and conditions of men. Well, then, it is just not enough to offer us the story of his death and resurrection. That makes it only a tenth of a tale, and we must know the rest.

No one ever called you a credulous fool, or Silvanus either, so you cannot help but see what I mean. Yet you tell me nothing of all this, and I suspect the reason must be that you do not know yourself. Well, then, my friend, get to know. The facts are still there, hidden in Jewish memories, to be gathered. May it not be that this sudden and unwelcome change in your fortunes gives you your chance? You are a born artist with a pen as well as with a paintbrush. Can it be that to collect all this information and to preserve it in a book is the particular task that the great God is laying upon you? Think it over. At any rate, to write to you like this is better than to drown you with sympathy, though truly I am deeply sorry for what has happened. Damn that infernal Issachar! But he may turn out to be just what you Christians need at present, a spur to goad you into a necessary change of direction. Stranger things than this have happened, and plotters are often trapped in their own snares.

LETTER EIGHTEEN

Silvanus to Luke

I AM actually staying in your old house in Street of the Herbalists sitting in your chair and writing at your table. You never did believe much in private possessions, did you? Not many men have so few of them, and hardly any other man I know would simply have wandered off to Troas, leaving his sparse furniture and his household goods behind him, and handing them over as gifts to his landlady. I suppose you felt that chairs and tables and pots and pans were encumbrances, brakes upon your freedom of movement, and so you simply abandoned them, like a snake sloughing its old skin and then slithering away through the dust without a single glance at what had clothed him for a whole year. That is not a very complimentary simile, I know. I had meant to write, 'like a snail growing a new shell', but I couldn't remember whether snails have this engaging habit of annual self-renewal. Perhaps, now I come to think of it, a snail is hardly a more flattering comparison than a snake for a man singularly unlike either creature.

But I perceive that I am drivelling aimlessly. It must be due to my subconscious desire to put off embarking seriously on what I know must be a very long letter. Let me say what I deeply feel, that staying in Luke's house with Luke not there, and worshipping with Luke's friends while he is miles away, is not exhilarating. Yet there may soon be a remedy for that which I will unfold in its due place in this letter, but much else must precede it.

Well, then, the good news first! We have at last settled this persistent and wretched problem of the relationship of Jew and

Gentile in the church of God, and on terms which the Gentile applauds and the Jew, though a little sadly, accepts. In other words, what you have always stood for and what Issachar and his wretched friends tried to deny is now the official practice of the church. You have won and they have lost. Issachar and his precious League may still cause trouble here and there, but their intransigence will die with them, and we have made it impossible for them ever again to claim that they have the support of James and the Elders and Apostles in Jerusalem.

Let me tell you the story for I cannot find that anyone else has yet done so. The first news I had of your departure and the scene which caused it came quickly in an almost incoherent letter from poor old Nicholas, who was outraged and anguished, ashamed and furious—all at once, and in every sentence. So I reported to James what had happened, got from him a firm denial of the use Issachar had made of his name, and went at once to Antioch to see what I could do. It was a sorry state of affairs that I found, but when I was able to deny that James had ever ordered that circumcision must be a pre-condition of baptism, that did something to restore the situation. Then it happened that Paul and Barnabas came back much sooner than was expected, and you can imagine that Issachar's influence began quickly to wane. Paul had a stirring tale to tell of the church in Cyprus, but he made it plain that he had not demanded circumcision from any of his converts there, and that if he had there would have been few of them. At a meeting of the church Issachar was repudiated, those he had led astray apologised and made their peace, and though I am not innocent enough to suppose that the spirit of faction, once raised, is as easily buried as that, yet old friends who had quarrelled were friends once more, and there was deep sincerity in the universal penitence which the brethren offered to God and also to Paul. Issachar and his friends discreetly vanished from Antioch, and Paul and Barnabas and I stayed there in order to strengthen the brethren by helping them to understand afresh and at a deeper level the glory of the liberty in Christ of which, by their baptism, they had been made free to accept.

It was several weeks before news of Issachar's next move reached us. I might have known that whoever else had repented of what had happened, he had not. He had hastened to Jerusalem, and there he had formally appealed to James and the Apostles, asking them to declare that circumcision and obedience to the Law of Moses was an obligation for all Christians, whether Jewish or Gentiles, and a necessary condition of baptism. Of course they refused, as he knew very well that they would refuse. But he calculated, rightly, that they would also hesitate to make a formal act then and there to release all Christians from the Jewish Law. They told him that a matter so weighty could be settled only by a General Council of Christians in Jerusalem, to which representatives of all other churches must be summoned. This suited Issachar very well for of necessity several weeks must elapse before the Council could actually meet, and this would give him and his friends time to work upon the racial pride and susceptibilities of the Jerusalem Christians, who were bound to be in a majority at the Council, and nearly all of whom were Jews. Thus when the formal summons to the Council came to the church at Antioch, and with it a private letter to me from a friend in Jerusalem describing how skilfully and indefatigably Issachar was using the breathing space, it behoved us to waste no time. A man would be a fool who underrated his powers as a propagandist, and nobody in Antioch who had seen them at work could deny them. So Paul and Barnabas and I left at once, and travelled to Jerusalem as fast as we could, leaving dear old Nicholas yet once more in charge of his beloved congregation. I wish you could have seen his broad, moonlike face, all beaming with satisfaction. It would have made up to you for a lot. He was much torn between a determination to love Issachar in Christian charity as was his duty, and his natural desire, as a natural man, that Paul would tell him exactly what he thought of him, without sparing him any of his fertility of denunciation. But he wanted to be present to hear it.

We found the brethren in Jerusalem very confused and uncertain of their duty. Not only are nearly all of them Jews, but some of them were trained as Pharisees, and had behind them all the long legal training of the Pharisee and all his instinctive championship of the Law. They are Pharisees still, or think they are. It is really important, my friend, that you should try to understand them, and judge them with charity. If you fail to do this you fail also to take the full measure of Paul's immense achievement and originality, and the price he has had to pay for it. Hardly any Jews who became disciples of Jesus ever imagined or could have imagined that this step separated them from the main stream of Jewish life, history, and thought, centred as it is in the veneration of Moses and the Law. If they were Pharisees before, they remained Pharisees after their baptism. Having been members of their synagogue all their lives, they saw no reason to relinquish their membership when they entered the church. Only to Sadducees was accepting Christ an obvious and clean-cut break across their lives, because they hold firmly that there cannot be any resurrection from the dead. The Sadducees therefore knew well that for them to follow the Way meant an absolute breach with their previous calling and history. The Pharisees, and others like them, only discovered this little by little and few of them have fully realised it even now. Yet it is so, or has been made so. Think, if you will, of this distressing controversy as their final struggle to avoid the break in the continuity of their lives. It is, for them, their own 'Agony in the Garden'. A man whose life is split in half, and who must cast off the whole of his history and his racial inheritance, is in a very tragic position. It was Paul's originality that from the first he saw this clearly and faced it creatively—and paid the heavy price. The rest of us Christian Jews are finding that whether or not we were intending to separate ourselves from Jewry, Jewry is firmly separating herself from us. You cannot reasonably expect the Christian Jew to accept all this without a desperate struggle of conscience.

So, you see, Issachar had plenty of ground on which to get a purchase. He could find painful and sensitive consciences in plenty, and for the skilled and not over-scrupulous propagandist they form ideal material. Therefore it seemed best to hold a preliminary and private meeting of those who could reasonably be thought of as the leaders of the church in order to settle, if we could, what policy we should recommend to the whole Council. This James agreed to do, and he and Peter, Paul, Barnabas, and I, and all the remaining Apostles who are still in Jerusalem were present. We began with a long period of silent prayer, asking the Holy Spirit to show us his will, and to give us the grace to speak all the truth as we saw it, but in love. There was in fact a great deal of very plain speaking, but all of it was charitable. The case for maintaining the separation between Jew and Gentile which the Law decrees was once more urged. So was the case against it. But it was the logic of events, not of principle or expediency, which finally brought us to be all of one mind, and the missionary experience of Peter and Paul was accepted as pointing to only one solution. They had had so much more to do with the Gentile world than the rest of us, and they testified emphatically that almost every Gentile they had brought into the church would have refused to come if circumcision had been the condition of his entry.

That was impressive but not by itself convincing. You know well how effective Issachar's obvious reply to that would have been. It was necessary for us to be sure that Gentile Christians had been welcomed by God with exactly the same generosity as Jewish Christians. To that question both Paul and Peter answered with an emphatic Yes. They both produced example after example of the fullness of divine grace coming equally and without any distinction upon Gentile and Jew when they had accepted Christ as their Lord. I added to that the argument that we were faced by a fact accomplished in that there are already more Gentiles than Jews in the church. Were we now to tell them that after all there had been something defective in their baptismal admission? We had recently seen at Antioch what happened when a young church was treated like that, and it was not an edifying spectacle. The same thing would happen elsewhere, and it was not possible to believe that this could be God's will. The grace given to the Gentile had been actually witnessed again and again. This was plain fact. It could not now be denied by us without our committing the sins of disloyalty to truth and ingratitude to God.

After that Peter finally clinched it. What was still needed was some final indication that the direction in which the debate was now so clearly moving was unmistakably due to the direction of the Holy Ghost. It was then that Peter related to us a vision he had been given before he 'went in with Gentiles and ate with them of unwashed hands', as he put it, at Joppa. He was hesitating to pay this price of ministering to the Gentiles, and in his vision God spoke directly to him, and said distinctly, 'What I have cleansed, that call not thou unholy'. It was of food unlawful to Jews that the voice had spoken. That settled it. There is hardly one of us who has not heard God speaking to us in a vision.

So it was that James, the man who least of all in that room could possibly be suspected of sitting lightly to the obligation of Jewish orthodoxy, rose at last to his feet and declared himself convinced that the Holy Ghost had spoken to us, and we must be obedient. At the Council he would recommend in our name that circumcision be not an obligation upon Gentile Christians, and that if they would abstain from eating the flesh of animals which had been strangled, from all flesh which had been previously offered to an idol, and would be faithful in alms giving for the poor, no further conditions could rightly be imposed upon them.

Then James rose slowly and stiffly to his feet. Unconsciously he made a ceremony of the movement. The most taciturn, the most reserved, the most respected of us all, who was never known to speak an idle or an unpondered word, was about to deliver the final judgement. 'For Jews', he said deliberately, 'it is a hard word, but for Gentiles a word of freedom. But we are entitled to believe that it is the word of the Holy Ghost. Twice at least he has spoken it, by the vision given to our brother Peter, and by the manifest, undeniable gift of grace to the Gentiles whom he and Paul have already admitted to the church. Here and now in our ears he has spoken again. This freedom from the Law of Moses we urge upon the Council because it seems good to the Holy Ghost and to us'.

James is an oracle. He is bound by ties of blood to the Lord as the rest of us are not. He used to be the most rigidly orthodox Jew among us. Of him alone it is true to say that when he speaks the judgement is declared and the case is finished. With Peter, one might argue, and Paul one might abuse, but few would care to argue with James, and fewer still to oppose him. The supremacy he has among us is his by right of character. So when the Council met three days later we had no doubt of what its verdict would be.

We met in the large walled open air court of the house of Joseph of Arimathea. About two hundred of us were present, and we sat on chairs arranged like a horseshoe, with James on a chair of honour, placed where all could see him. All round the walls the flowers were blazing, and they blended well with the vivid colours of the mosaic tiles of the floor. For these mosaics Joseph had spent a lifetime and a fortune scouring the world. We stood as James came in. We sang a hymn first, and then he led us in prayer, and afterwards our prayer for the guidance of the Holy Spirit was long and silent. I confess that I was very interested to see how James would deal with the whole situation. Would that most silent man rehearse the points of the controversy at full length? Or would he who finds speech so foreign to him call on others to speak for him?

Actually, he did neither. His was a wonderful performance, and the lawyer and advocate in me applauded it unreservedly. I could not myself have done at all what he did with brilliant success. He described why the Council had been summoned, and how it was that the whole future of the church might hang on its decision. He then put in turn the Jewish and the Gentile points of view, with a fairness so absolute that neither the stormy petrel Paul nor Issachar and his Law Defence League, who were sitting together in a corner collectively glowering, could possibly say that they were being misrepresented. And all this he did in less than ten minutes. It was so masterly a performance that I would hardly have believed a mortal mind could achieve it.

Then he called on Peter to state his case, and then on Paul. They both simply told what their experience had been and were content to leave it at that. I was afraid that Paul might go off into one of his long diatribes about the incompetence of the Law to do what it promised, that is to make holy a man who obeys it. Mercifully he did not, though even so there were mutterings of 'Traitor' and 'Renegade' from Issachar's corner. Paul does undoubtedly have that effect upon his opponents, even when he is studiously refraining himself from provoking them. Peter, on the other hand, can say exactly the same things, and nobody minds. It is an odd contrast they make. When James asked for any other delegate to speak his mind, Issachar treated us to a piece of his academic theorising, but he had no command over the gathering and he knew it. So he did not make the mistake of creating a scene. A few others then spoke briefly about how their own churches had dealt or failed to deal with the problem. But the mind of the Council was already so clearly made up that no one wished to hear any more, and James, who had been writing whilst the last speakers were on their feet, rose to test the Council's decision by reading what he had written.

It was the draft of a pastoral letter from the Council of Jerusalem to all the churches of Christ. He prefaced his reading of it by saying that the case for setting Gentile Christians free from the obligations of the Jewish Law seemed to him to be proved, and that there was a warrant for it in the prophetic writings. He therefore asked the Council to accept as their act and deed the letter he would read to them, and then to send a copy of it by the hands of chosen delegates of the Council to every church which had a mixed Jewish and Gentile membership. This is the wording of the letter:

The apostles and elders and brethren send greeting to the brethren which are of the Gentiles in Antioch and Syria and Cilicia. Forasmuch as we have heard that certain which went out from us have troubled you with words, subverting your souls, saying, Ye must be circumcised and keep the Law; to whom we gave no such commandment: it seemed good to us, being assembled with one accord, to send chosen men to you with our beloved Barnabas and Paul, men that have hazarded their lives for the name of our Lord Jesus Christ. We have sent also Jude and Silvanus to tell you the same things by word of mouth. For it has seemed good to the Holy Ghost and to us to lay upon you no greater burden than these necessary things, namely that you must not eat meat which has been offered to idols, you must not eat meat which has been cut out of a still living animal, or which comes from any animal which has been put to death by strangling. Nor must you commit fornication. Keep yourselves from all these things, and all will be well with you. Farewell.

You will note the phrase, 'To whom we gave no such commandment'. It was, and was intended to be, a public rebuke and a repudiation of Issachar and his League. Without a word, he and his friends stalked out. James let them go, saying no

word, but looking stricken. We have not, I fear, even yet heard
the last of them, for there was no trace of shame or penitence
in their gesture, but only defiance. The Council agreed unan-
imously to the letter.

It is very short. It contains only the minimum of what is
essential if Gentiles and Jews are to live together in the same
church. But it is the Great Charter of your freedom, and for
it you must thank the Jews since, as you see, it is they who have
done all the giving. It is, perhaps one of the most purely
generous gestures we Jews have ever made. Though the
accidents of my birth of very wealthy parents, and the liberal
education they gave me, have made a widely travelled cosmo-
politan of me, on that day, my friend, I was proud and thankful
to be a man of my own Jewish nation.

The next thing was to take the letter to Antioch. Paul, Barnabas, Jude, and I had been entrusted with this pleasant mission,
and Peter came along with us. We gathered all the church
together, and after the Eucharist Paul stood and solemnly
read the letter aloud. Some of the brethren cheered and some
wept with relief and joy. But all the time there was the unspoken realisation of a great absence. Luke was not there.
Nevertheless, there was joy over so great a deliverance, and a
clearly felt assumption that henceforward there would be no
more trouble.

I thought at the time that this assumption was a trifle naïve
and innocent. Once the spirit of faction is set free, it is not so
easily chained up again. Sure enough, it was not long before
the old trouble flared up again, but this time in such an absurd
way that no one would have guarded against it. The Roman
Servetus gave a garden party in honour of us five delegates
from Jerusalem and invited a large number of the Gentile
Christians to come to it. All was going very happily when
suddenly jeers and taunts rang out from behind hedges and
bushes. It was this infernal Law Defence League once again,

which had suborned brazen-lunged orators, and told them what to shout. 'Jews without lily-white hands! What a nice change!' one voice jeered. 'We'll tell the Lord Caiaphas about this, he *will* be pleased,' cried another. Then, more angrily, 'What price the Law now which you swore to keep?' The final taunt was well aimed, 'Look at dear old Peter, guzzling with his new Gentile pals. Go and be a Syrian, old man, and be done with it.'

That did it! Had they threatened, he had threatened too. But jeers could always suddenly unman him. He would be martyred tomorrow morning, gladly. But to look a fool? No, not yet; it's the humiliation he simply cannot learn. He blushed, he muttered some apology to his host, and he fled—and, alas, Barnabas fled with him. Nicholas was purple with fury, and Paul fairly stammered with rage. Some of us ran to search the grounds, but that was useless. The darkness of Daphne hid them. In great embarrassment the party broke up.

Actually it was no more than a very unpleasant storm in a teacup, a pin prick. Nothing that those ruffians shouted could alter the fact of the liberation proclaimed by the Council of Jerusalem. Nor did the scene they made make any difference to the restoration of fellowship in the church. Paul was there to see to that, and the Antioch Christians had had more than enough of strife and bickering, so that there never was any danger that they would be stampeded again.

The apostles themselves, as you can imagine, were not able to be immune from the infection of faction. Peter and Barnabas had, after all, come straight from the Council of Jerusalem as its official delegates, and then had publicly done the very thing they had denounced others for doing, and which the Council had repudiated. Paul, though God knows he tried his very hardest, could not help but be bitter, and to his face he told Peter how badly he had behaved. Some sort of peace was patched up between them, and then Peter went back to Jerusalem, which was the best thing he could do, and it did ease the situation, even if it did not wholly mend it. After all, Barnabas was still there, and he, Paul's special friend, had also gone back on his word. So there was a discomfort among us, and this came to a head when a new missionary journey to Bithynia was suggested. Paul leaped at it, as did Barnabas who assumed he would go with him. But when Barnabas wanted to take John Mark with them, Paul would not hear of it as Mark had once failed him in Cyprus. Barnabas fought hard, saying that he too had failed him not many days earlier. But Paul was adamant. He does not easily forgive failures of this kind. So our intrepid missionary partners have temporarily separated. Barnabas and Mark have gone to Cyprus, and in a few days Paul and I set out for Bithynia.

You see the point. Troas is not on the road to Bithynia but yet it is not impossibly far from it. I hope one way or another to come to see you. How I shall contrive it I do not yet know, but I have an inward feeling that you and I are soon destined to renew the springs of our friendship. There would be nothing in this world I could look forward to more than that.

Persis to Nicholas   TROAS
                                                         A.D. 51

HERE we are in Troas, and it's where we hadn't ought to
be—I know that. But we are, and I'll explain why we're
here and not in the wilds of Bithynia presently. We're in
Luke's house too, and we're all of us writing letters for dear
life, except Paul who's asleep in bed. In the surgery Luke is
writing to his high-up friend Theophilus in Rome. In the
living-room Silvanus is writing to James in Jerusalem. And I'm
in the kitchen writing to you. I thought Luke was supposed to
have gone to be a hermit. Well, this hermitage isn't any dusty
hole in a desert or a damp cave in a mountain. Its a commodious
and well-appointed modern residence, as the house agents say.
All this letter writing is a bit too like a last will and testament
business for my liking, and when I look out to sea and at the
hills of Macedonia beyond the straits, and think that we're all
going there tomorrow in a little ship which doesn't look at all
safe to me, well, I get cold feet. God knows what's waiting for
us all over yonder—stonings, beatings, prison, death may be.
But what's the odds? If it must be it must be, and we're in for
it now. I expect I'll be sea sick too.

But, Nicholas, I'm having adventures. *Me*, a fat little man
with a bald head and sore feet who's spent all his life with his
backside glued to a chair, writing letters for people like you
for two denarii a page. Whoever would have thought it!
And, do you know, I'm really enjoying it. I wouldn't have
missed it for worlds, sore feet and all. This chap who's been
fording flooded rivers, shoving Malachi the mule along the
edge of precipices, shooting arrows at wild deer for food,
and hitting some of them, scouting ahead or doing rearguard

in the dangerous bits, is *Me*, Persis the Scribe. I can hardly believe it myself.

I'm getting the low-down on these missionary tours, and finding out all the bits that Paul and Barnabas don't think to mention when they come back home and tell us all about the Cypriots or Cilicians they've converted, and the trouble they've had with the Jews, and all the riots they've been in. When Paul asked me to go along with them and act as secretary to the expedition, I thought it would mostly mean writing their letters and looking after the money and buying the food, and things like that. So it has, but it's meant a lot more too that I never bargained for. It means endless walking, trudging along for mile after mile, baked to a cinder one day and half-drowned the next, and leading the mule one minute, and then getting behind and shoving the pigheaded son of Beelzebub. Some day, perhaps, I'll find out how to make mules do what you want, but so far this one (I call him Malachi) only does what *he* wants, and one of the things he wants is a lot of rests, and they have to be long ones too. As long as you are on one of the main Roman roads it's easy. Perhaps you join up with a merchant's convoy. That makes a nice change, except that the merchants probably have camels, and Malachi doesn't approve of camels. When he isn't sidling up to one to bite it, he's either running like fury to get away from them or else he's dawdling and stopping all the time. The language I've used about him! I'm sure Christians oughtn't to say such words, and I didn't know I knew them!

As long as you're on the roads, it's not too bad. There aren't any snakes and there aren't any brigands, and there's always a Public Rest House at the end of the day. Some of them are good and some aren't, and a few are fairly hopping with fleas. But you aren't always on the roads, not if you're making for a place like Bithynia, so you have to strike across country, and either the rivers are dry so you can't get any water, or else they're flooded so you can't cross them. Then mountains get in your way, so you have to walk for miles along narrow paths beside deep precipices. Malachi doesn't like precipices either! There might be brigands, and there's certain to be snakes. It's all very hair-raising, and your feet get sorer and sorer, but how you sleep at nights.

But we're a cheerful party. Silvanus generally strides ahead on his long legs, singing Latin poems when he's in good form, which he mostly is. Paul and Timothy generally walk together talking and talking. We picked up Timothy in Lystra, and brought him along with us. Malachi and I generally bring up the rear, Malachi carrying the gear and me leading him. Sometimes he bolts, and then he leads me and we get in front, me tugging at the bridle and Silvanus laughing at us as we shoot past him, shouting some snappy remark from Catullus or some other poet to cheer us up.

We got to Derbe first, and then Lystra, and then we left the roads and made a bee-line for Bithynia. We headed across country, and we should have gone almost due north. But we never got there. It was a dreadful journey. We didn't seem to be able to do anything right. If we came to a river, it would be certain to be flooded so that we couldn't ford it, or if there was a bridge the span would be broken so that we couldn't cross it. So we'd have to turn west again and follow the river for miles till we could find a place to cross it. Whenever we tried to go north something went wrong and stopped us. Whenever we went west, everything, including Malachi, seemed to go right. After a couple of weeks of this kind of thing, Silvanus said one night, 'You know, it doesn't look as if we were meant to go to Bithynia'. For a time Paul would not listen to such talk. He had set his heart on visiting the churches in Galatia. So on we went again, and the more we struggled to make progress northwards the more the stars in their courses seemed to force us to move westwards. After one more week of it

Paul himself collapsed with another dose of his old trouble, and he was very poorly. So he gave in at last, and agreed that it really did look as if the Holy Ghost was determined not to let us go to Bithynia. After a day or two's rest, he was fit to travel again, but he had to ride on Malachi, and we had to carry Malachi's load between us. When all this happened we weren't very far from the Troas road, so we decided the best thing to do was to get Paul to Troas where he could be examined by Luke the physician. I never saw a man more indecently pleased at being blocked from his goal than Silvanus was when we decided to go to Troas instead. And the odd thing was that immediately we'd taken the decision, Paul began to get better in the most astonishing way. He was walking for most of the last day's journey, and by the time we got to Troas, he was perfectly fit. Luke looked him over for form's sake, and he made him rest and take it easy for a week, but, as he said, there was really nothing wrong with him any more.

So now you know why we're here and not in Bithynia. It was really lovely getting to Luke's house again, and I'll never forget the look on his face when he opened the door and saw his old friends—a sort of Am-I-Dreaming—Or-is-It-Really-True look. It was a wonderful evening of explanations and news, with a marvellous supper, extra carrots for Malachi, and a soft warm bed for all of us. We'd earned it, I thought.

Well, then we had to have a council of war. There didn't seem much to do in Troas, and we weren't to be let go to Bithynia, and we didn't want to go tamely back to Antioch. So what were we to do? Then it was that Luke took a hand. 'I'm a Greek' he said, 'and a Macedonian. Look through the window. You can actually see the Macedon hills. Has the Way been taken across the strait to Macedonia? God knows, it needs it, and badly. Why not go there? If you do, I'll come with you. Paul needs a physician to look after him'. Then he read us a long letter from his high-up friend in Rome. What this man was saying was that a religion intending to conquer the world mustn't let itself be cooped up in the backwater of Asia Minor. It must follow the Roman roads to Rome. 'From here', said Luke, 'the obvious way to Rome is through Philippi in Macedon, and then westwards through the rest of Greece'. Silvanus said that it sounded good sense and good strategy. Paul was silent for a bit. Silvanus guessed what he was thinking, and said gently 'After all, you know, Bithynia is really Peter's ground'. So then Paul agreed, and they all embraced and blessed each other, and we said our prayers about it. Still it seemed right. So here we are, and we're off to Macedonia in the morning, leaving poor old Malachi to be looked after by a friendly inn-keeper. I hope I'll see him again some day. I've really got rather fond of the obstinate old devil.

Luke to Theophilus   TROAS
                                                              A.D. 51

(Only the latter part of this letter is quoted here, for its chief
purpose was to make Theophilus aware of the events described
by Silvanus and by Persis in the last two letters in this collection.)

. . . SO you see, dear friend, the heavy weight of fruit your
letter has borne. Few letters accomplish so much. By refusing
to pour pity over me you saved me from self-pity; and in the
circumstances I have already described to you you see how the
reading of your letter persuaded Silvanus who needed little
persuasion, and Paul, who needed a great deal, that your views
of the strategic necessities of the church are right. So tomorrow
we set sail from the same little harbour where centuries ago the
ships of Agamemnon, Menelaus, and Ulysses anchored for the
Siege of Troy and lay in the bay for ten long years. To me there
seems a certain rightness that the first expedition of the spiritual
invasion of Europe should set out from the same historic spot.

What may be in front of me I cannot know. Paul is the only
man in our party who has much experience of these missionary
expeditions, and he leaves one in no doubt that they can be
dangerous, and that beatings and imprisonment are the certain
fate of those who take part in them. I suppose it is likely enough,
especially in a city like Philippi, our first stopping place, which
is notorious throughout all Greece for its wickedness. To
persuade people to forsake an old religion and accept a new
one claiming to be exclusively the Truth must plainly be a risky
occupation. But somehow I don't anticipate anything much
worse than discomfort, cold, weariness, and hunger, the insults
and taunts of angry crowds, and the occasional night or two

in a bug-ridden cell in some local prison. It's not a big price to
pay for the joy I've been freely given, and one can't expect
to launch the true Faith on the waters of a hostile world
without pains and penalties. If you are right, as I believe you
are, the price we shall have to pay in the next few months is
likely to be as a very little thing compared with what will be
demanded from our successors of the next generation when
this Way begins to undermine the corruptions of Rome herself.
In any case, it is fully time that I faced a little discomfort. It
ought to do me good for up to now my life, though busy, has
really been shockingly soft and easy.

But I don't plan to give the whole of the rest of my life to
this kind of work. If I am really to accept your suggestion,
which was also and independently mine since I made it to
Silvanus, and write down in order all the facts of the Lord's life,
I must obviously go to Palestine for it is in that distressful land
that these facts lie hidden. In these last few days, I have had a
great deal of talk with Silvanus and some with Paul about it
all. They leave me in no doubt of their belief that it is a task
which urgently needs to be done, that I am in many ways
qualified to attempt it, and that I must regard it as having been
truly laid upon me by the Lord's will. I cannot find any good
reason for not accepting this view of theirs, and of yours too.
The fact that my own inclination points me to the same purpose
is not a reason for doubting the genuineness of the divine
vocation. So I have my marching orders and with God's help
I will obey them.

Why, then, you may ask, am I going with Paul and Silvanus
into Macedonia tomorrow, instead of to Palestine? Partly it
is because Paul has been ill recently and needs a physician by
his side for a time. But chiefly I go because I want to watch
Paul at work, and to see for myself just how the church takes
root in a heathen city, and grows there. You see, it is not very
logical to write fully of the life of Jesus and then to end the

story abruptly with his death and resurrection and ascension into heaven. That is to suggest that his work came to an end on the day he left the world to return to the Father. It is also to suggest something quite false about himself, namely that he was another of the heroes, greater by far no doubt than any before him, but still of the same stuff as they. And that is not the truth, and because it is not I shall be false to my charge if I content myself by writing a book about a dead hero. The whole point is that he is not dead, but living now and for ever, not quiescent but intensely active now and for ever in and through his church which Paul, in a most suggestive phrase, calls his body on earth. Paul, indeed, is always emphatic that whatever virtue, praise or glory there may be in the church's adventure is the Lord's praise and glory. Whatever help we may give to the world is his help. Our work is his work, and it is he himself who is really doing it all the time. Because of all this I really plan a book of two volumes—the first, the life and teaching of Jesus, and the second, his activity in the church. So I have to see a little of the latter for myself.

How or when I shall get to Palestine I hardly know, but I have no doubt that I shall. There may be dangers as well as discomforts ahead, but if God really wants me to write this book then he will somehow make it possible. All I have to do is to take this next step and then trust him for the rest.

For that matter Palestine tomorrow may be just as dangerous as Greece today, though in a different way. Silvanus confirms what you wrote in your last letter. There is certainly a rebellion against Rome in the making. He thinks the plot will not be ripe for a few years yet, but he is convinced that the day of its poisonous fruition will come. I hope it may not be until after I have done my work there and left the country, as I hope, for ever. For not even the fact that it is the land of the Lord's nativity makes me take kindly to Palestine. But all these things will happen as they must, and if it turns out that I have to conduct my researches into the Lord's life in the middle of a battle, so be it. I should ask you for a safe conduct.

Did you know, by the way, that Jesus foresaw the coming revolt of Palestine and prophesied that it would end in the total destruction of Jerusalem? I did not until Silvanus told me of it yesterday. It is an excellent illustration of what may be lost to the world unless someone collects all these sayings. It seems that when he knew the time of his sacrifice was near, he set his face to go to Jerusalem where, he knew, it would be accomplished. Coming to it from the north you see nothing of the city until you have climbed to the top of the last hill, and then, suddenly, you see it all, for it is spread beneath your feet. At this summit large crowds met him to escort him into the city in triumph, Silvanus was there himself and saw the Lord and heard what he said. For Jesus, when he saw that great city, turned away from his cheering escort, and gazed at it long and sadly. The tears filled his eyes as he cried aloud, 'Jerusalem, Jerusalem, if thou hadst known, even thou, at least in this day given to thee, the things belonging to thy peace. But, as it is, thou canst not see them. The day will come to thee that thine enemies will dig a trench around thee, and encircle thee, and keep thee in on every side, and shall bring thee down, level with the ground, and thy children within thee. They will not leave in thee one stone upon another, and all because thou didst not recognise the time of thy visitation'. One had been the poorer not to know that. It is just the sort of thing I must search out when I get to Palestine. But Macedonia first, and from there I hope to write to you again. And so farewell, and God keep and bless you.

INTERLUDE

(The correspondence here leaps over a gap of 4 years, until the Travellers, their several evangelistic journeys at last accomplished as the scriptures tell, reassemble together at Troas, whence they had set out. Like a greater than he before him, Paul knows he must steadfastly set his face to Jerusalem, and so their second departure from Troas is more sombre than their first. It is at this point that the correspondence begins again.)

PART TWO

Theophilus to Silvanus   ROME
                                                                 A.D. 54

IN the last four years I have heard too seldom from you but a good deal of you. Luke is one of my sources of information for he writes from time to time to tell me what is happening to him, and through him I get some news of you and of Paul, who, as you know, I have never met, but I hope I may. I have heard recently that he is planning to undertake a journey to Rome, and from there to the western extremity of the Empire in Spain. I hope this is true for many reasons of which the first is that if you come with him—and you seem seldom to be very far away from him—then you could stay with me, and we could verify, so to speak, our old friendship face to face. But if this should happen at all, then you must try to bring Luke with you. I count on you, Silvanus, to do this. It is much, much too long since I last saw him. The last time was in Athens, ten or twelve years ago, and that, as you will be the first to agree, is far too long to be deprived of the sight of the most charming and companionable of all men. Be sure, then, to bring him too.

Do I need to dangle baits before you both? No, but if I did I should say (and it is the truth) that though I am learning much about the Way of Jesus of Nazareth, more about how the church proclaims it, I still seem to know very few Christians, and those whom I do meet from time to time do not seem able to answer the particular questions I want to ask. You will have heard of Andronicus here and his wife Junia, since it is in their house that the church in Rome often meets for worship. Well, I've known them for years and am very fond of both of them, as anyone who knows them must be, for theirs is the perfect marriage, and, believe me, to see the perfect marriage

in Roman society is nowadays a rare event. Just occasionally,
and in an uncommitted way, you understand, I have been
their guest when their Christian friends have come to them
for prayer and worship, and I have been honoured by an
invitation to stay and join with them. Their obvious sincerity
and their apparently unquenchable joy in it all impresses me
deeply. So does the untiring way in which they care for each
other, and their creative sensitiveness to all the suffering they
see. Whether the sufferers are Christians or not seems to make
no difference to them. Whatever the cost to them may be,
they never fail to do everything they can to alleviate it, and this
resolute, steady caring for unhappy people is a too rare spectacle
in modern Rome. But though I deeply admire them, I don't
think I could be close friends with many of them. You will be
thinking that I am not very far from the church of Jesus myself.
Well, perhaps I am not. There is something in the life of these
people which deeply attracts me, and then my old friendship
with Luke and yourself draws me too. But I must be sure of
myself, and there are questions I must have satisfactorily
answered before I finally commit myself, and I think that only
you two and Paul can answer them. Come, then, to my rescue,
all three of you.

You see, the price I should have to pay for my conversion
would be a very heavy one. The Emperor has woken to the
fact that this new religion is not just one among so many
others. There is a certain exclusive particularity about it, and
he is now beginning to realise this. Being, as he is, most far-
sighted in all that concerns his own authority, he sees in the
followers of Jesus of Nazareth the faintest shadow of a threat
both to himself and to the stability of the State. At present
there are too few Christians in Rome for it to be worth his
while to take any action. 'But they need to be watched', he
said to me only yesterday. 'We must find out how fast they are
growing. This Jesus called himself a King, didn't he? In Rome

there is only room for one monarch, and that monarch is myself'. There was a hard and ominous light in his eyes as he said it. He has asked for copies of all the police reports of Paul's doings in Philippi, Athens, Corinth, Ephesus, and elsewhere. Of course, as you will realise, they come to me automatically as imperial minister of state, which is how I, in my turn, have been able to follow you all as you have moved about the empire from place to place. I shall have to send them, but I shall take the risk of suppressing the report of the riot in Ephesus over the images of the Goddess Diana. Then, as I was about to back myself out of the imperial presence, he suddenly glanced at me with that sidelong look of his, and said, 'By the way, Theophilus, perhaps it would be better if you, in your position, went less often to your friends Andronicus and Junia when the Christians are in their house'. That was all—a friendly warning more than a threat—but I can be certain that I shall be watched.

I once wrote to Luke that if the Christians wished to win Rome, as they must or else lose the world, they would have to pay a heavy price in blood and suffering. The early ominous signs of it have already appeared in the sky. What I did not realise at that time was that I myself, if I do become a Christian, will certainly be one of the first to do the paying. I am ready for that, but only if I am sure that this Way is the truth, and that it has the power to cure Rome's corruption. I must be certain first. Come soon, all three of you, and instruct me.

I MUST reply to your very welcome letter immediately and therefore briefly, together with a promise to write fully as soon as we arrive at Jerusalem. For it is to that city, not, alas, to Rome, that we are bound. All of us are still travelling together, Paul, and Luke and I, and that brave and humorous little man Persis, the public letter-writer of Antioch, who for the last four years has been acting as the secretary, the treasurer, and even the caterer of this long missionary tour.

We have need of his humour for, to tell the truth, this has now become a dolorous journey. Paul is quite determined to go to Jerusalem, and nothing will shake him. He does not doubt, as none of us doubt, that disaster waits there for us. If we had entertained any delusions about that the laments wailed over us by the Christians in every port at which we touch would by now have dispelled our optimism. Everywhere they crowd round us and weep over us, and beseech us to give up this mad journey. We go to our death, they say; and they tell us of this plot and that to kidnap Paul and kill him to which one section of the Pharisees or another have bound themselves with various fearsome rituals. Indeed, it may well be so. No Jew on earth is more bitterly hated than he. To disagree with him seems to be to hate him, and to start hatching plots to discredit or to assassinate him. It is odd that it should be so. I too am a Jew, a lawyer, and also a Christian. Whatever Paul has done I have done too, and yet, so far as I can gather, no Jew has sworn to spill my blood or die in the attempt. Yet Paul is actually more lovable and much more loving than I can ever hope to be. He is also far, far more effective. No one would think me worth the trouble of silencing. But desperate efforts to silence Paul have never ceased since the day of his conversion on the Damascus Road.

So our progress is punctuated by tears and farewell speeches. None of it makes the least difference to his resolve. It is with him as though he had some inner compulsion to be obedient to a strange destiny. Luke and I agree that it is certainly a strange one. What, we ask each other, can he hope to get out of Jerusalem but beatings and riots and humiliation? What chance has he of achieving anything? His apostolate is to the Gentiles. He has always said so, and has formally turned his back on the Jews again and again. Yet he cannot leave them alone. Always he is turning to them just once more for one last try. I suppose it must be that in spite of all he is more ineradicably a Jew than I am, and the wound of his rejection and our Lord's by their own race has struck deep and never been healed.

Sometimes voices speak to Paul in the night, and when they do he is always obedient to them. He has no doubt whence they come, and nor have I. They have told him lately that while in Jerusalem he must be bound in chains for the Lord's sake, he will nevertheless not be killed there, since he must eventually go to Rome to bear his final witness. He believes this implicitly, and indeed so do I, especially the first part of the prophecy. We should reach Jerusalem in less than a month, and there we shall step straight into certain trouble. I wouldn't mind if I could see what good it was going to do. But there! I have written that before, and after all, which of us can see all the ends of our ventures? The main thing is that we should not be disobedient to our heavenly visions. Luke takes all this rather more cheerfully than I do, for he has his own purpose in Palestine, to gather information about the daily life there of our Lord, and no one can doubt the use of that.

So you see Paul plans to come to Rome—when he is allowed. Luke plans to come when Paul comes, provided his work is

finished first. So it looks as if you may have to wait for a year
or more for a sight of either of them. If this should turn out
to be so, then I will come myself as early as I possibly can, and
without waiting for Paul and Luke. I badly want to see you,
and someone must try to answer the questions you write of.
But first I must be sure that Paul is safe, and beyond the reach
of the High Priest and his multitudinous conspirators.

LETTER TWENTY-THREE

Theophilus to Felix, Governor of Palestine   ROME
A.D. 55

IT is well known and appreciated here that Rome has no
abler or more experienced Governor in all the Empire than
yourself. You have long wielded the imperial authority in the
most difficult of all provinces, and with greater success than any
of your predecessors. It may seem a little superfluous, therefore,
for me to write to you a friendly and informal letter of warning,
but believe me that it is a measure of my high regard for you.
I would not permit myself such a liberty unless I were sure that
you would not construe it as a criticism.

I have reason to believe that very soon and very suddenly
you will be faced by a highly dangerous and explosive situation
in Jerusalem. With your long knowledge and experience of
the Jews, you will have heard about Paul of Tarsus, the ardent
Pharisee who became one of the foremost of the Christian
Leaders. You will know better than I what a stormy petrel
he is, and how passionate and unyielding is the hate of him
in the breasts of all orthodox Jews. Wherever he goes trouble
at once arises, and yet it is the rancorous Jews who cause it,
not he.

Some of his close friends, particularly Luke the Physician
and Silvanus the Lawyer, are also very old friends of mine.
I have letters from them telling me that Paul is now immovably
determined to go to Jerusalem. They say that more than one
plot is hatching to assassinate him, while various dissident
groups are plotting to bring him to some sort of trial which
will enable them to observe the outward forms of legality
and yet force the hand of the Roman authority to execute
him. Other letters from our secret agents amply confirm

all this. The same technique used in the case of Jesus of Nazareth is apparently to be repeated for the benefit of Paul of Tarsus.

Who will know better than you how skilled these Jews are in all the arts of the propagandist? Yet I venture to urge upon you great wariness and caution. Their tactics in the case of Jesus were to present Pontius Pilate with a choice between an unjust condemnation of the prisoner and a failure to keep under control a skilfully maddened mob. Pontius chose to execute the prisoner, well knowing that he had committed nothing worthy of death, and, worse, having actually said so publicly. In the dilemma he was caught in at that moment any of us, I suppose, might have made the same choice, though I hope we should not. But then he ought never to have allowed himself to be edged into such an impossible position. That is what these Jews will try to do to you, but you must not let them. If Paul is arrested, as almost certainly he will be, you will then have to hear the case. But there is no legal reason why you should not transfer the hearing to Caesarea, and thus force the prosecution and the witnesses to come to you, with heads a little cooled by the journey. A trial for blasphemy, as the Jews will call it, is almost impossible to conduct justly in Jerusalem, without precipitating the very trouble we Romans must avoid.

Though this Paul has friends who are friends of mine I am not obliquely pleading for any preferential treatment for him. He must naturally be tried by Roman law without fear or favour. Nor am I pleading for any exceptionally merciful treatment for him because he is a Christian, even though I know several Christians and deeply respect them and their religion. What I am pleading for is the fair name of Roman justice, which in Palestine was badly compromised by the weakness of your unhappy predecessor Pontius, though in your governship, as we all know, it has been steadily vindicated. But the real test may now suddenly come upon you, and of this I venture to warn you, and beseech you to act both with speed and with great caution. These Jews are wonderful propagandists, and you must keep your thoughts several moves ahead of theirs.

Luke to Theophilus   CAESAREA
                                                          A.D. 56

WE have been pausing here for several days to get a little
rest before going on with the last lap of our journey
from Troas to Jerusalem, and facing whatever waits for us there.
So far our progress has been along the Via Dolorosa, and made
mournful by farewell speeches in every place, by prophecies
of doom, by tears, and by dramatic warnings of disaster.
'What mean ye to weep and break my heart', Paul exclaims
from time to time. But nothing turns him from his purpose.
Though the skies fall, to Jerusalem he will still go, and tomorrow
we go with him. The danger is for him, not for us, which is
all the more reason why we must not leave him to face it alone.

So while I can, I write to you. What is there in this Paul, you
ask in your last letter, which wins the devotion of men like
Silvanus and Luke? You find it hard to understand since to
you he seems pig-headed, troublesome, and generally in-
tolerable. I am not surprised. That will certainly be the
impression likely to be made on a Roman administrator who
has never met him. But when you do meet him (for he himself
is eager to meet you and is firmly convinced that events will
so fall out as to make this meeting possible) you will find yourself utterly repelled or completely charmed. There never are
any half measures about people's views of him, for he is the
kind of man who is met either by love or hate, but never,
never by indifference. Silvanus and I, who know and care
deeply for you both, are sure that you will be charmed by him.
We have noticed many times that everybody who meets him
is decisively the better or the worse for the encounter. Speech
with him is for most a turning point in life, and the moment of

meeting him is a moment of fateful decision. In this power to challenge inexorably he is more like his master Jesus than any of the other apostles.

He is without exception the most single-minded person I have ever known. For this reason he is also by far the most effective. He has a will like a battering ram and a backbone like steel. The determination to destroy the Christians root and branch, and the determination to spread the Christian church throughout the world, are not contradictions. They flow from the same constituents of character and are served with the same inflexible and selfless resolve. Both as persecutor and as founder exactly the same concentration of all resources upon one single aim are brought into play, and this is always the first condition of real effectiveness. The church will never know a more dangerous enemy than he was, nor yet a more powerful friend than he now is. In both capacities his meteoric progress has naturally caused disturbances and trouble to civil authorities wherever he has been. Let him but appear on any scene and riots seem inevitably to occur, but they followed him before he was a Christian, and not only after his conversion. The stoning of Stephen in Jerusalem was after all a riotous occasion, 'prejudicial to public order', as the police put it. It is true that public order and Paul agree ill together, but that is no fault of his, and in any case the values he serves are of even higher importance than civil peace and quietness.

Just a fanatic! you observe with distaste. Yes, certainly a fanatic, and ordinarily I dislike the breed as heartily as you do. But Paul is what at first sight seems like a contradiction in terms, a lovable fanatic. You must take my word for this. I know the man intimately. I have seen him in his least as well as in his most attractive moments, and I admire him deeply and love him profoundly. Ineradicably Greek as I am, and therefore distrustful of all fanaticism, and ineradicably Jewish as he is, and therefore so predisposed to the emotional and the extreme;

yet we have a warm, settled intimacy, and are at our ease in it. From him I draw a steady fixity of purpose to do what I can to serve the Lord, and were it not for him I could never have it. From me he draws—what? An understanding of his nature, I think, and a realisation of his tremendous importance in Christian history, and, yes, a certain compassion which, I hope, is neither superior nor enervating.

For Paul is a man who needs compassion. This may sound strange to you when you remember all I had written in this and other letters about his tremendous strength. But it is true. You see, he is very sensitive. Direct insults he can bear and quickly forget. He has many times been beaten, and though such an ordeal hurts him physically just as much as it would hurt any man, he takes it rather as the schoolboy who is caned by his master. The stripes are on his back, not on his mind, and he quickly puts them behind him. But when he is let down by people for whom he has cared, when he is spurned by those whom he admires, when the love he freely gives is thrown back in his face, then he is hurt so bitterly and deeply that it often brings on a recurrence of his fever, and he is prostrated for days. No judicial beating has ever done that to him, but the wounds of his spirit have often done it. But what he feels most deeply of all is when his own Jewish people, and Christians at that, follow him round from place to place and deliberately set themselves to disturb and unsettle some new young church which he has founded and given the whole power and genius of his pastoral love to build. This is nothing less than sheer agony for him, and it is an agony he has had to bear not once but many times. Indeed I do not believe that there is a single place where he has preached the Gospel where this has failed to happen. So much of his life, poor man, is passed in agony of spirit.

And he is a Jew, an intensely patriotic Jew, and it is the Jews and only the Jews who do these things to him, and they do it

out of personal spite, and a hatred never to be assuaged in this
life. There is the real tragedy. Never was man prouder of his
nation than Paul is of his Jewish ancestry. He happens to be a
Roman citizen, but that is a little thing to him when put
beside his Jewish blood. It is the Jews he loves most, and they
spurn him. The Jewish religion is what he really wants to reform
or fulfil, and it has failed him. Naturally he loves the Gentiles
too, but much less intensely, and yet they rise to him and welcome him. He is entangled in a subtle trap of his own, a love-
hate relationship with his own kith and kin. By a kind of
divine appointment he is the apostle of the Gentiles, chosen
specially among the apostles to serve them. He does so with
all his power—but much of his heart is permanently with his
own people. Always he is looking over his shoulder at them.
Always he is returning to them to 'have one last try' to make
them see the wonder of what they are rejecting. The last try
inevitably fails, and he cries, 'You judge yourselves unworthy:
I turn to the Gentiles'. But he never can completely cut himself
free from the Jews. There is always the thought at the back of
his mind, 'Will not my own people turn and believe, even
now?' And so he tries yet once more and is again met by
insult and hatred. That is exactly what he is doing at this
minute. He will accomplish nothing by this journey to Jerusalem. That is to say, he will not succeed in winning for the
Lord the loyalty of his own people. In his heart he knows it,
and yet he must go, for he is driven by a kind of daemon.

With the Gentiles his life is one long triumph. With the Jews
it is blank, total, unrelieved failure. In the long perspectives of
history only the triumph will be remembered for almost every
non-Jewish church owes its foundation to him, and he is destined to be, has in fact already become the father of the Lord's
Gentile children. He would rather be the father of Christian
Jewry. So it is that this, the most effective and for history the
most influential man living, with a power of giving and attract-

ing love which I have never seen paralleled, is also a man who
calls for a very deep and steady compassion. It is necessary for
him and for his work that some friend of his, who can give him
the compassionate understanding he needs, should always be
with him. He needs his circle of discriminating friends, and
I am one of them, and know that in this crisis I must be at his
side.

But that is not to say that I agree with everything he says,
or even see in this Christian Way the same values which he sees
in the same order of importance. That letter of his to the
Christians in Rome which Junius showed you is a very good
example of what I mean. You say that though there are some
parts of it which make your heart leap and thrill, yet, taken as
a whole you find it largely unintelligible. I too have seen and
studied that letter, and like you I find it most difficult to understand. There are parts which are glorious: 'Who shall separate
us from the love of Christ', for instance. And the last part of it
which is full of practical advice is common-sensible and straightforward if a trifle pedestrian. But the rest of it is a document
which is almost absurdly difficult, and, furthermore, one which,
when at long last I have managed to understand it, neither re-
flects nor illumines any experience of my own. In other words,
he is not thinking in my categories of mind or speaking to my
conditions, or to yours, or to any Gentile's.

For it is written by a Jew and addressed to Jews, and no one
but a Jew has the kind of experience necessary to interpret it.
The whole of the long argument about the Law must be almost
meaningless to anyone who cannot give to the Law of Moses
the full depth of reverential meaning which no one but a
Jew could be expected to give. But Jews understand 'The Law'
as meaning little less than the word of God; and Paul is
struggling to find suitable words to say that what he, in
common with the rest of Jewry, once taught as the direct word
of God to his nation, has proved in his experience to be a kind

of cheat or impostor. His painful and detailed obedience to it did not give him what he was entitled to expect and what it promised, the achievement of holiness and the sense of freedom from sin. Far from that, it did the exact opposite, it made him twenty times more conscious of his sin than he would have been without it, and it produced in him a sense of moral impotence against which he raged endlessly and helplessly. Hence of course, his theory of justification, or forgiveness, by faith in Jesus, of which the letter is so full. But his love-hate relationship with the Jews comes in here too. He cannot simply say, as you and I would say, 'The Law has failed me and cheated me, therefore it is bogus, and I shall have nothing more to do with it'. No, he must always be turning back to it time after time, and arguing endlessly about it simply because he cannot bear the thought that what is life itself to his nation should have become a dusty emptiness to him, the most loyal of its sons.

Though I understand what that letter of his is trying to say and why it takes the form it does, I am like you in thinking much of it bizarre and exaggerated. Yet that fact does not in the least undermine our friendship, and you too, when you meet him, will find yourself charmed by the most lovable and attractive of men. You, like myself, will delight to be in his company. But though I delight to be with him, as, I think, he finds it a happiness to be with me, the strange truth is that the influence we have over each other is very limited. His life and mine started from the furthest ends of human experience and racial tradition. Then in the fullness of time, when our characters were fully adult and our ways set, our two lives came together, merged, and coalesced in the sharing of a supreme experience of God in Christ Jesus our Lord. So we are at one in religion, and that unity is much deeper than the separation of nationhood and training. We share fully a common gratitude to Jesus. We know that we are both forgiven for all our sins by his mercy and through his cross. We acknowledge ourselves bound by a single overriding obligation to spend our lives in spreading the Lord's kingdom. In addition to all that we are tied together both by the compulsion of circumstances and by the thraldom of a common human attraction.

Few men are bound so close as he and I. But none of that alters the fact that our characters are quite different. Both of us are convinced Christians, but I can no more cut myself off from my Greek past than he can from his Jewish past. And so we see this same Christian Way from different points of view. We do not see the same values in it, or at any rate we see them in a different order, and in many aspects of the bearing of the Way on human life and its problems I find myself at one with Silvanus, who has shed so much of his 'Jewishness', and at odds with Paul who has shed none of it. That is not to say that we quarrel or even argue. Each of us assumes his own point of view and respects his partner's.

He is obsessed by a sense of moral impotence. 'The evil that I would not, that I do, and the good that I would, that I do not'. It is a quotation from that letter of his which sticks in my mind. But that is because I have heard him say it many a time. It seems honestly to surprise him that he is not yet perfect. But I cannot take it so tragically. I do not expect to be perfect in this life, and the forgiveness of sin by God means for me a release from the sense of guilt, which saves me from being obsessed by it. Paul is a moralist, and a rather narrow one. Look at that perpetual cataloguing of various sins which occurs in one letter after another of his. He writes them all down, time after time, as though they shocked and astonished him. But I cannot make myself feel shocked or pretend to be much astonished by them. Perhaps that is the physician's training coming out in me. They happen because of our weak human nature, and they have to be dealt with. But compassion deals with them much better than denunciation could ever do.

And forgiveness, coming as it does from the compassion of God, is, it seems to me, a blotting out of sin, and that ought to save one from worrying about it any more. The fruit of forgiveness ought, surely, to be an imperturbable serenity of spirit, but it is hardly that for Paul.

Yet for me as for him sins exist which, by making us furiously angry, destroy serenity. But they are not the same sins. Neither of us is, or ever was, an adulterer or a homosexual. But while the mere thought of such things rouses in him a passion of disgust, I can take them quite calmly. What rouses me to fury is cruelty in any shape or form, or the delight in wielding power over any other human being, or the withholding of compassion from those who suffer before one's eyes, or the insensitive assumption of the rich that the possession of wealth automatically confers moral or social superiority.

I am not saying that Paul fails to repudiate these things. He does, but he is not eloquent about them any more than I am eloquent about the sins of the flesh, which in my turn, I repudiate as he does. The difference in our moral codes or instincts is probably due to the fact that to him has been given the charge of many churches, while I have no responsibilities of that kind. And it is the plain fact that adultery will wreck the community life of a church much more quickly than hardheartedness even though it is the lesser sin, and so the pastoral administrator cannot help but be specially sensitive to the former, even though he may know very well that Jesus himself would regard the latter as more worthy of condemnation.

But for what purpose, after all, are we founding these little churches of the Lord in one town after another? To provide the Lord with his body on earth Paul would say, and I should say so too. But that is to furnish in and for every place a visible community to exhibit his spirit and display his power. A church and every member of it is to be judged, I believe, by whether the true spirit of Jesus is to be seen in it or not. For me that is the crucial and vital thing about the Way, and all else is quite secondary and unimportant. But all this assumes that we know beyond any shadow of doubt what the spirit of Jesus was and is, and until the whole church knows far more about how he lived, what he taught, and what he did than it seems that we know now, we cannot be sure that we have caught more than a whisper of his Way. But the church cannot know this until someone finds it out and writes it down in a book. That is my next task. More than that, it seems to me to be nothing less than the supreme purpose for which I was born into the world. This sounds too presumptuous to write of to anyone but you, and to speak of to anyone but Silvanus. But you and he who first bound me to the task will understand, and at least you will see how seriously I regard it.

P.S. I have read this letter again and it seems a disgracefully self-centred document, which never so much as mentions the joyful news of your drawing nearer to the Way of our Lord. Dearest brother, I do very greatly rejoice, and I hold you up to the Lord for blessing every day in my prayers.

Felix to Theophilus   CAESAREA
                                                                A.D. 56

I VENTURE to add this private letter to my official Report
on the case of the prisoner Paul. It is to thank your Excellency
sincerely for the personal warning you wrote to me. Paul was
not in Jerusalem so much as one week before his presence
caused a riot in the Temple and he was under arrest. But
because I had your letter in time, I was able to write to Lysias,
our centurion in Jerusalem, to warn him of what might happen,
and to order him at any cost to guard Paul from all danger of
harm by mob violence. Thus he was very quickly on the spot
when the riot began, and he put him under protective arrest
at once. He allowed the briefest possible preliminary hearing
of the case in Jerusalem, and then, when the accusation of
blasphemy had been made, he immediately adjourned the hearing to Caesarea, where the prisoner could be brought before
the Governor himself. Such was the emotional disturbance of
the whole country which this man Paul had quickened, that
Lysias had to take extraordinary measures to make certain of
his safety. He sent him here with an escort of nearly 500
soldiers. I would like warmly to commend to your Excellency
the conduct of Centurion Lysias. He was faced with a very
difficult situation, and in it he conducted himself with a firmness,
a prudence, and a care for justice worthy of the highest
traditions of Rome. The facts that the prisoner is safe, and that
the Jews have sent no complaint to the Emperor about the conduct of the Roman authorities, are a high testimony to the
skill and resource of Lysias.

The rest of the story your Excellency will read in my
official report. But it is an unfinished story. My term of office

here is about to end, and in a few days I am to be relieved by
Porcius Festus. I have written to him to make him aware of
the special circumstances attaching to Paul, and to warn him
against allowing any trial of him to take place in Jerusalem. He
has replied to tell me that he fully appreciates the position,
and he has undertaken to keep him in safety in Caesarea and to
hear his case here. But he says that it may be some little time
before he can do so because King Agrippa has meanwhile
written to him to ask him to postpone any trial until he can get
to Caesarea to hear it himself. How King Agrippa comes to
be so interested in Paul I do not know.

Meanwhile, Paul is held under sufficient restraint to guarantee
his safety but not under the close penal restraint of a convicted
felon in a prison. He lives comfortably in a private house, but
he is guarded day and night, and is forbidden to make speeches
in public when he walks in the street with his guards. His
friends may visit him as and when they wish. Luke the Physician
constantly does so, though he is now beginning to travel more
widely about Palestine to further some business of his own.
Silvanus left here months ago, I believe for Rome, where you
may already have seen him.

I shall be more than sorry to leave Paul behind me. I have
seen much of him and talked often with him. He impresses
me deeply and I am getting very fond of him. There is something unusual about him, and he is a far, far bigger man than
he looks. But I am sure that my successor will continue to make
his condition of arrest as unburdensome as is compatible with
his safety.

As I now come home after so many years as Governor of
Palestine, I should wish to thank your Excellency for your
continuous support and help which has never failed me, and
also for the kind words of praise you felt able to write to me.
I have striven always to uphold Roman justice, and to govern
this difficult people for their own good.

Philip the Deacon to James the Apostle and Elder   CAESAREA
A.D. 56

YOUR Lordship will perhaps have heard from our brothers
Paul and Silvanus that my daughters and I have our
Gentile Christian brother, Luke the Physician of Antioch,
lodging with us. He came here with Paul, whose devoted
friend he is, and he intends to make his home here for so long
as Paul is held in captivity by the Romans, which, for reasons
you already know, may be for many months. To him Luke
ministers almost daily, and he is of course a member of the
church in this house, and a great comfort to my daughters and
me in these troublous times.

Luke has a plan, of which our brothers Paul and Silvanus are
aware and approve of, to find out all he can about the life of
our dear Lord and to write it all down in a book. He says that
unless someone does this while the people who knew him are
still alive there is danger that all the knowledge we have, and
is so precious to us, of what he taught and how he answered the
Pharisees, will be lost. If it is lost, those who come after us will
know no more of him than that he was the son of God, who
was unjustly crucified and rose from the dead on the third day.
So, at any rate, Luke says, and though it is hard for us to believe
that any follower of Jesus should know as little of him as that,
I suppose that he may be right. And, rather to our surprise and
our shame, neither I nor any of my daughters can answer
more than a few of the questions Luke asks us about him.
Being a physician he is especially interested in how he cast out
devils and cured diseases like leprosy and palsy, and he asked
us to give him a list of the people Jesus had healed, the diseases
they had, and how he dealt with them. We found that we could

only remember a few of them at all clearly, and we knew that there were many more of which we knew very few of the details, and some which we had not heard of. Then he asked us many questions about the Lord's birth. We knew that there was a good deal of mystery about it, but not what the mystery was. In fact we could not answer him; nor could we tell him anything about the Lord's boyhood. 'Already it seems', we said to him, 'our memories are failing us'. 'Yes,' he replied, 'people's memories do fail or play them tricks as they grow older, and that is exactly the point'.

He is sure that he must travel about the country for a time, seeking out all he can find who knew the Lord and asking them to tell him everything they can remember. But he thinks that many of them will be cautious in these dangerous times of speaking freely to him, as a Gentile, unless he has some kind of written authority to show. He asked me to write him a letter, and I would gladly do it, but I do not think my name would carry enough weight. I wondered about our brother Paul, but I am afraid that his signature on such a letter at this present time would be as likely to close mouths as to open them. So I wondered if your Lordship would be so kind as to write a short letter which Luke could show as evidence that he has the authority of the Lord's own brother and the elder of the church to ask his questions, if, that is, you approve of his purpose as Paul and Silvanus have done. Luke is a most worthy follower of the Lord, and I guarantee that he would not abuse your trust.

My daughters and I and the church in Caesarea send our respectful greetings to your Lordship.

LETTER TWENTY-SEVEN

James the Apostle and Elder to the Christians   JERUSALEM
of Palestine whom it may concern   A.D. 56

TO our beloved brethren in Palestine, Greeting in the Lord. The bearer of this letter is our most worthy brother Luke, the Physician of Antioch, a learned and discreet follower of the Lord, in whom we place our full confidence. He has undertaken a mission at the bidding of the Apostles and elders of the church to write in a book all that is known of the life of our Lord among us. To this end he must ask many questions of those who had the privilege to meet and speak with the Lord. This is to testify that in this he has our full authority, and to ask all those to whom he presents this letter to answer his questions fully and freely, and to do all in their power to help him.

James: Apostle and Elder.

LETTER TWENTY-EIGHT

Luke to Silvanus   <small>EMMAUS</small>
<small>A.D.</small> 57

AN account of my travels of the last nine months and of
such discoveries as I have made is overdue, and it is to you
that I ought to send it as a thank-offering for the encourage-
ment you always gave me to undertake this task. For nine
months now I have been travelling slowly and leisurely about
this land. I have had Persis with me as companion and secretary,
and he, refusing to be parted from Malachi the mule, brought
him along to carry the baggage. Malachi's manners much
improved these days, and were he human (and at times he
almost seems so to us) he would join us both as we send our
greetings to you.

Armed with a letter of introduction from James, we have
travelled desultorily from place to place. Our first plan was to
start at Nazareth in Galilee, as the Lord's boyhood home, and
then to follow his footsteps point by point until at last we came
to the fatal Hill of Golgotha. It was a logical plan in theory,
but it was useless in practice. It proved to be quite impossible
to take a map of Palestine and trace on it in due and logical
order a line showing the route he took. Already people's
memories of dates and places have become confused and
unreliable. They remember clearly enough that one day he
healed ten lepers, on another he cured a man of palsy, and they
remember, too, much of what he said in this discourse or that.
But ask them when and where he did or said these things,
and either you get no answer at all or else the answers contradict each other. Therein lies much of my difficulty. It is already
too late to write down in proper, accurate order the things
the Lord said and did; and whatever my book turns out to be

when I have at last written it, it cannot be what we Greeks understand by a work of history or biography. It must of course have a definite shape and form, for otherwise it could not be even a narrative. But the narrative's pattern must perforce be imposed upon the facts by the author, who will have to be as much the interpreter as the historian or the biographer. Naturally, and let me hasten to avow it, that does not absolve the interpreter from his primary obligation to be scrupulously faithful to the facts of the Lord's life and teaching. But there is now no hope at all of arranging all these facts, which lie between the baptism of the Lord and his final entry into Jerusalem, in the exact order in which they actually took place.

I must then look for truth of a different kind, and the shape the process of search has taken suggests of what kind this is. A man in Jericho, say, tells me something, and then says that a woman in Caesarea Philippi can tell me still more about it. So we go from Jericho to Caesarea Philippi, where this woman passes me on to a farmer in Bethsaida whose pigs were drowned when the Lord healed a lunatic, while he in turn tells me the name and address of a publican down in Galilee who heard the Lord tell the story of the Prodigal Son. I follow all these trails in turn, always trying to hear of people still living whom the Lord is known to have healed, or, it may be, forgiven, and then going perhaps a good many miles out of my way to get from them their memories of what actually happened, and the impressions they formed about it. Then from time to time I have doubled back to Caesarea, from Jerusalem perhaps or Sidon, to see how Paul was faring, and to have a few days' rest in Philip's house.

It has been a wonderful, unforgettable journey. Think of it, Silvanus; I have climbed the mountain near Caesarea Philippi, where Peter acknowledged the Lord as the Son of the Living God, and where, a little later, he was transfigured and the glory of heaven clothed him. I think, I am almost sure, that I found

the exact spot, a grassy cup high on the mountainside, where
flowers bloom in greater profusion than anywhere else I have
seen in all this land. That my feet should have stood where his
stood then! That I should have sat on the very rock where he
sat then, gravely listening to Peter's stammering of the incredible truth, and then pointing to the inevitable consequences
of that truth—'The Son of Man must suffer, must be betrayed,
must be killed'. There are some experiences indescribable and
unforgettable, and that was one of them.

Happily Palestine is full of inns and inn-keepers. They are
not only convenient for travellers, but have proved to be the
best sources of information, I found a lively and cheerful inn-
keeper at Jericho, for instance, who knew the story of the Good
Samaritan just as well as I did. Do you remember telling it to
me that day when we were both in the prison at Philippi?

'Do you mean to say', I asked him, 'that that was a story of
what actually happened, that the Samaritan brought the
wounded man to this very inn?'

'Well, no sir, not quite like that', he replied. 'But he easily
might have. It wouldn't have been the first time that we've
had a wounded man here who's been robbed and battered by
the gangs of brigands haunting the road to Jerusalem. We've
always tried to behave decently to them too'.

'Then you think that Jesus might have had this inn in mind
when he told the story?'

'I don't know about that, sir,' replied my host, 'but he very
well might have. You see, he came to this inn once or twice;
and I remember telling him about one badly hurt man as was
carried in here on a litter'.

'Then you knew him', I said. 'Are you a follower of his?'

'Well, no, not actually,' he replied, 'I can't say as I am.
Keeping an inn doesn't leave you much time for that sort of
thing, as you might say. But I've often wished I was. He was
a good man, you see, and always so kind and considerate, and

there was something about his eyes you'd never forget, not if you lived to be a hundred. We always loved it when he came here, and while he was in it, and for long afterwards, the house was a better place. And I've never believed the things those Sadducees and Pharisees said about him; nor I can't bear to think about his end. But maybe it wasn't his end. There's them as says he's living still. But I've never seen him again.' Well, that inn-keeper is a Christian now. I baptised him myself.

And now I am writing this from another inn, at Emmaus, a day's journey north-west of Jerusalem, as you will know, where I have got on to the track of an event of the first Easter morning, which I believe that neither you nor Paul have heard of. It appears that two disciples were travelling that morning, hopeless and broken in spirit, towards Emmaus, when, suddenly, the risen Lord caught them up and walked with them, but they did not know who he was. He talked to them, and comforted them by showing them how essential it was that the Lord must so suffer, but still they did not know him. Then they came to this inn, and when the stranger broke and crumbled the bread for their supper, they suddenly realised who he was. He immediately vanished, as it were behind the veil of their senses, and they returned at once to Jerusalem to give the news to Peter and the other apostles. The same man keeps the inn to-day, and it is from him that I have had this story, which I have checked as best I can from other sources, and have no doubt it is true.

So it has been all over the country, I have found the man whom the Lord healed of the palsy. I have hunted out two of the ten lepers he cured; the others being now dead or untraceable. I have discovered a publican in Samaria who was present when the Lord told the story you once told me of the Prodigal Son and his graceless brother. I have met another publican in Jerusalem whom the Lord saved from the sins of extortion and avarice. I have talked with all kinds of people who sat at his feet when he taught them. I have found many witnesses of the miracle of the feeding of five thousand people with five loaves and a few fishes. All these, and many, many more have added their mites to the growing and vivid picture of the Lord at work in the hills and valleys of this beautiful country.

But on many points it is difficult to reach certainty. The most unimpeachable eye-witnesses are so apt to contradict each other on matters of detail. One such point has cropped up about the Last Supper. When people are prepared for baptism, they are always taught about the Last Supper, how the Lord assembled his apostles, how he broke bread and called it his body and gave them wine and called it his blood, and how this bread and wine, when consecrated, are to us nothing less than the very life of God himself and the symbolic assurances of his presence with us. So much every Christian knows. He may well be ignorant of some of the healing miracles and of some of the Lord's parables, but he will assuredly not be ignorant of the Last Supper. It is like the Crucifixion and the Resurrection, a fact universally known and received among us.

Yet when trying to find out the other facts about what happened in the Upper Room on that night, I came across clear contradiction of evidence. There was the unhappy quarrel among the apostles about which of them were going to hold the highest positions in the new kingdom, and this was rebuked and settled by the Lord when he ceremonially washed their feet. But did all this happen before the Supper or after it? I had always understood that it happened before the Supper, and that the Lord felt he must restore their harmony before the Supper could be allowed to begin. But I have come across very good evidence, as it seems to me, that it happened after the Supper was finished, and before they all went into the Garden of Gethsemane. According to this evidence, the Supper was over, the quarrel began, and the Lord rebuked them by washing their feet. Then, when they were feeling unbearably ashamed he said the most surprising thing to them.

'But be comforted. You are the men who have stayed steadfastly at my side throughout all my trials; and I *have* chosen you for high position in my kingdom, for there you will eat and drink at my own table, and you will sit like kings on thrones, judging the twelve tribes of Israel'.

There is an irony so terrible in that that I am sure it must be true. For those steadfast men were in a few minutes all to fall asleep when he had expressly asked them to watch over him while he prayed, and in a few minutes more all but one were to bolt for their lives, and that one, having tried to defend him with a sword, would that same night twice deny that he ever knew him. But it is the actual evidence, not the dramatic irony of the scene, which convinces me that the sequence of the events on that night must have been so, and not exactly as we were all taught.

If I were to tell you much more about my travels and discoveries I should find myself writing a book rather than a letter. I will not weary you, or myself, by inflicting any more detail on you. Besides, I have not yet had time to meditate upon it, so that it is still undigested and ill arranged. For this reason, and for another I will put before you at the end of this letter, I am nowhere near ready to expand my notes into a book.

But there is something I want to write to you now, and to ask you to tell me what you think of it, since you, after all, are my elder brother in the Way, and yourself began to follow it while the Lord was still in his human flesh. No man could spend the last nine months as I have spent them, with his whole mind and purpose concentrated upon the effort to find eye-witnesses of the Lord's life, without gaining in the process a freshness of view of the Gospel he has been taught and in which he lives. Let me say at once that I have discovered nothing which in any way modifies, much less changes, that which is basic in the whole of the apostolic preaching of the Gospel. He came forth from God. He died for our sins. He rose again to open the Gate of Heaven to us. He ascended in triumph to prepare a place for us. I believe that as completely today as I did a year ago. Nay, I believe it if possible more completely, because every single new piece of knowledge about the Lord which has come my way, reasserts, guarantees, and underlines this basic and essential Gospel.

But the frame of this central picture of God's act to secure man's salvation has changed for me. It is far fuller and richer than it was, and the effect of the new frame is to alter and enrich for me the values of the Gospel, not for my eternal salvation or yours, but for the mission and work of the Church in history in the here-and-now world. I think I can only make plain what I mean by outlining to you the ways in which my search has given me a picture of the work and purpose of Jesus, about which I cannot remember having heard much from my previous teachers in the Faith.

I have never before realised how incessant was his thought and teaching about the Kingdom of God. Naturally I had heard of it, but I had always supposed that he meant Heaven. It now seems absolutely clear from the testimony of scores of witnesses that Heaven is only a part of what he meant. The Kingdom of God is for this world. He came to bring it to this world. He told some people that they could enter it here and now, others that they had already entered it, others again that they were not far from it. I suppose (and I pray) that he would say that you and I and Paul and Persis, and all the rest of us are actually in this Kingdom now, exercising our citizenship all the time. But at the same time there is that other strand in his teaching about it, namely that the Kingdom of God is not here yet, and has still to be won. That is what the church exists to do. The Kingdom of God exists, and yet it does not exist, it is here, and yet it is also far away. But its coming is certain, and the world will be saved and become as Heaven. The only real question is, How long, O Lord, How Long?

I cannot discover that he ever defined it more fully than this, nor, for that matter, in quite such terms as these. He was not a logician or a philosopher. But the meaning which I put on it is that the Kingdom of God exists now wherever there is a circle of men and women who are trying to live under the obedience of God in Jesus' power and for his sake. As those areas of the holy obedience, now but islets in a vast ocean, spread and merge, so the Kingdom grows.

If this is the picture of the Gospel in action which the Lord intended to impress (and I can find much to confirm it and nothing to contradict it) then we have a frame into which almost every detail of the Gospel story can be fitted. He offered a kingdom, and a kingdom implies a king to rule and a community to serve. When I began to realise how much of the Lord's teaching was devoted to explaining the Kingdom of God, it astonished me that I had heard so little about it before. As I look back to my days in Antioch where I first became a Christian, I cannot remember that it was ever much mentioned. Perhaps this may have been because so many of our teachers there were sure that the world was very soon to end—a hope, or a fear, which I never did believe. Still, if you think that the world may cease to exist at almost any moment there is every point in struggling to convince all who will listen that their sins can be forgiven, and that eternal life awaits them. But thinking and talking about kingdoms will seem rather pointless. Paul does not envisage any sudden or imminent ending of the world. Far from that, he spends a good deal of time gently rebuking those who do. Yet I don't think I have ever heard him use the phrase, the Kingdom of God. But this was certainly the phrase which the Lord used far more frequently than any other. I find this omission very strange, and I don't understand it. Do you think that Paul doesn't know that the idea of the Kingdom of God was the corner-stone of all the Lord's social and ethical teaching? Or is it some kind of blind spot in him?

I must ask him some time, but not until he is in the mood to welcome such a question!

For me the discovery has been a revelation. It is the new frame of the Gospel picture. In the Lord Jesus I found from the first a hero to worship, but until now I was never quite so sure that I had also found a cause to serve. Into this frame every detail of the picture fits and makes a consistent and harmonious pattern. Everything that I knew about the Lord before, and everything I have discovered lately, can be held together round the promise of the Kingdom of God, just as every part of the human body is held in its position by the backbone. The Gospel is more than the Kingdom, but it is the Kingdom and the King which make its backbone.

The training of the apostles is plainly the training of men who must be the first architects of a kingdom. The healings of the sick are the signs and evidences of the presence of the King in his Kingdom. The Lord's moral teaching always has the social undertone which makes it the ethics of the kingdom. The sins most constantly rebuked—trust in wealth, lust for power over other human beings, the corruption of the innocent, self-indulgence—are always the sins which most offend the kingdom. The virtues—kindness, charity, humility, an imaginative and adaptable sensitiveness, trust, and expectancy, are those which make most possible the new life together of sinful men and women in the kingdom. And again, in the Lord's view of it, the mark of having entered the Kingdom, is that one claims and is ready to die to assert not the precious uniqueness of one's own personality, but that of all the others, separately, freely, and equally.

I am, as you see, on fire with all this, but I think it is a fire which will burn within me as long as I live, for I feel like a man whose eyes are at last wide open, having been at first and for many years blind, and then, for the last few years only half open. I have been converted again. Now I know what I am about, what my life is for. I realise what the real purpose is that I must serve in this book. For the increase of the Lord's kingdom I continue with my search. 'Thy kingdom come', he taught us to pray and I believe that I can best hasten its coming by writing, not too worthlessly, this book of the Lord's life and ministry among us, but for this I must still search long and far. I have not yet found out anything like enough, as is shown by the obvious holes and gaps in the narrative I have so far outlined.

The most serious and obvious gap comes at the beginning of the story. Has it struck you, Silvanus, that we know almost everything about the end of the Lord's story and almost nothing about its beginning? By the humiliation of the Cross and the miracles of the Empty Tomb and the Hill of Ascension he returned to God. But what of the day when he came from God? Miracle was in that advent, and humiliation too. But what were the forms or signs of it? I know the rumours. I hear them everywhere. But to get the evidence which confirms them and sifts them is another and a harder thing. Those who should know guard their tongues and veil their speech, as though they had a vow of silence laid on them. Perhaps they have. If the rumours point to truth, the reticence of the actors automatically follows. Thus I may have to face the old question of the historian's conscience—should so natural a desire for privacy be respected if it means the concealment or the loss of knowledge which the following generations ought to possess and make known? If I am successful in the next stage of my search I may find myself wrestling with that dilemma of morals. For I am clear that I must at any rate try to confirm or deny the rumours, and tomorrow I go to Bethlehem where the Lord was born since it is plainly there that I am most likely to get on the trail of knowledge about the events which surrounded that birth.

Luke to Silvanus   BETHLEHEM
                                                             A.D. 58

MY last letter was written to an old friend. This is to the same friend because he is a poet. I might have written it to Paul, or to my Caesarea host, Philip the Deacon, or even to Theophilus. They would all understand the story I have to tell for, superficially, it is just a narrative like any other. But its undertones are the purest poetry and only a poet will discern them. Already you will see that I am more excited; even more exalted in spirit than I have ever been before; and as I am about to expose myself it must be to a friend who has the imagination of an artist and the sympathy of a poet, since he alone will understand.

What would you feel like, Silvanus, if you were poking about in an old burial ground in Salamis, and the dusty roll of parchment you unearthed with your stick turned out to be the full text of one of Euripides' lost tragedies? Though exceedingly unlikely, it is not impossible. He is known to have written more than we now possess, and Salamis would be the likeliest place to search. Again, what would you feel like? At first there would be the catching of the breath in a wild surmise; then incredulity, banished only by the searching, microscopic scrutiny of every word in the text; and then a sense of tremendous awe that this incredible chance should have happened to you, and with it a realisation of the really frightening responsibility now laid on you. Luck like that would hardly come the way of more than one man in the world in a century, so the day you found it would be the one wholly unforgettable day of your life, a day unique, unlike any other that went before it or came after it.

Take the element of chance out of that simile, and it is exactly what has happened to me. I have before me on my table as I write a document more important by far than all the tragedies of Euripides and Aeschylus put together, and the sheer grace and lyric beauty of which makes me catch my breath for joy, and surpasses any writing I have ever read before. It is the full story of what can be told and made public of all the strange circumstances surrounding the Lord's birth. It was given to me freely to use as I would in my book, but on condition that I made no attempt to discover who wrote it. Neither I nor any other Christian will ever know the author, and I take my pledge to ask no questions to include a restraint even on private curiosity and guessing. It was written in Hebrew and by someone who had no other tongue. Its language is rough and pastoral, its thought forms and idioms are Hebrew through and through, and it simply will not 'go' into modern grammatical Greek. I have vainly tried to translate it into the sort of Greek that you and I, or Euripides too for that matter, would write. The only result is to ruin it. That would be literary treason indeed, for in its original Hebrew form the story is told with a graceful charm which is unique and incomparable. I cannot translate it without robbing it of all its distinction of style, so I must simply transliterate it from Hebrew to Greek, word by word and phrase by phrase. There is no other way to keep its distinction and character intact.

I endured many days of vain and wearisome searching here in Bethlehem. Though the Lord belonged to Nazareth in Galilee, he was born here. Everyone knows that. All know further that the birth took place in the cattle byre of the inn, as there was nowhere else Mary could go when her pains took her. It is in this inn that I am staying, for there is no other in the village. We have all heard rumours, too, about shepherds being led by a star to the place where he would be born. But apart from this, Bethlehem seems to have figured very little in the Lord's ministry, and therefore all the questions I could ask had to be about the circumstances of the birth. I could not lead gradually up to what I wanted by asking first what had happened, say, to old Jeremy whom the Lord had healed of his paralysis. But ask as I would, no one would answer. All were polite, kind and welcoming. They would talk freely on any other subject, but on this, No. Some were evasive, some frankly embarrassed, most hurriedly disclaimed all knowledge. No shepherd would admit to having been present on that night. The inn-keeper, son to the inn-keeper of that day, showed me the cattle byre, where I knelt in worship. Though it is genuinely a cattle byre, and used still for that purpose, there is a moving sense of fragrance about it. But it was as though he had a mandate to show the byre, and a prohibition to go one inch further. To all questions he smiled and shook his head. James' letter of introduction was for once useless. There was an impalpable blank wall, and the letter could not penetrate it.

So I continued for several days until I was so weary and disappointed that I was about to give it up, and go back to Caesarea. Then late one evening, when the inn's customers had gone home and all was quiet and still, the inn-keeper came in to me, and asked if he might talk.

I was sitting in my wooden chair writing a letter on the clean scrubbed table, for this inn, as is fitting, is kept clean, fresh, and sweet. The room has white walls and two large shuttered windows, and at night it is lit by a couple of candles on the table, and a hanging oil lamp near the door and another over the hearth in which, that night, a dung and wood fire was burning. The inn-keeper is a man of about forty—tall, dark, and bearded, not given to much speaking, and having a statuesque quality about him. He can be active when occasion requires it, but he has the unusual gift of stillness and immobility. It is the quietness of controlled force, not of inertia, and it creates confidence. Besides, if he is silent, his eyes are kind. He came in and stood there, he was wearing what I always call his Joseph cloak, for it has many hues and shades, gold, scarlet, blue, brown, and green, woven together in great broad bands of colour. The cloak, lit up by the steady light of a hanging oil lamp above him and the leaping flames of the fire in front of him, seemed to dance and shimmer like a haze of colour. Every detail of that scene is vivid in my mind, and it always will be.

In his hands he carried a large rolled scroll of parchment. It was clear that he intended to make a ceremony of what was to come, for he bowed before he spoke, and his expression was grave but kind. The words he used he had rehearsed in his mind, and he spoke them with the steady, slow precision of an actor in an Athenian play.

'Sir', he said quietly, 'I ask your forgiveness for disturbing you, but I have been sent to offer you the answer, or so much of it as may be told, to the many questions you came here to ask. In this scroll the story is written by one whose name you must not ask, but who knows all the facts and certifies that everything written here is true. There are two other copies of this scroll, but none of them has passed outside this valley or been seen by anyone not immediately concerned with the events it describes. It is a secret paper, the talisman of a mystery, and I am one of those appointed to guard it. We, the guardians, have watched you while you have been here. We have seen your patience under disappointment, and have noted your gentle courtesy with those who had no choice but to refuse answers to your questions. We know you to be a good man and a true follower of the Way, and we have checked on impressions by making various enquiries about you and the mission laid on you. And so we have decided to entrust to you this knowledge, and to lay upon you the task of making it known to future followers of the Way. For they ought to know it for their faith's sake, but not until all those whose secrets it tells have passed to their eternal reward. So I am commanded to give you this freely and gladly, making no condition as to how you use it. But before I hand it to you, you must make to me two solemn promises. The first is that you will never try to discover who it was that wrote it. The second is that you will not allow its contents to be generally known through your book for five more years. Do you formally give these promises and solemnly swear that you will keep them?'

I hesitated for a moment. I was being asked to make promises about my use of a document I had not read. But the first promise seemed reasonable, and the second easy since no one knows so well as I that there is no hope of my book being finished within five years from now. Moreover, if these people, speaking through the inn-keeper, are ready to trust me, I ought to trust them. So I thanked him warmly and made my promise. He handed over the scroll, and blessed me, and bowed himself out of the room. I spent the rest of the evening reading it, and went late to bed, my mind a turmoil.

I must not begin to discharge my trust by immediately breaking my promise, even though no one in the world can be more safely trusted with a confidence than you. So I cannot do what I most long to do, that is to send you this scroll and share with you my discovery. Nor must I tell you in too much detail what is in it. But I think I can write to you about it in general terms, and tell you just enough of its contents to make what I write intelligible.

Broadly and roughly, then, it is the story of the intermingling of the two family circles into which Jesus of Nazareth and his cousin John the Baptist were born. That Jesus was born of a virgin is made perfectly plain. His blessed mother did not marry her husband until after he had been conceived, and Joseph, for his part, did not put her away as at one time he had been minded to do. But strange circumstances heralded John's birth, too; and both these births were announced by the visitations of angels. Such is what is essential in the story, but the many details which I have omitted make it very clear that God deliberately intervened in the normal course of things to cause both these births. Elizabeth was too old for childbearing; Mary was a virgin, and to both angels appeared, announcing their strange destinies, stating that they were sent from God, and saying that on these two children the whole fate of Israel would turn.

Now, as you know, I have in recent years read widely in the Jewish scriptures. In thought, in feeling, in expression, this whole story before me is informed by their spirit, not only at its best but far beyond the best that any of those old writers achieved. But the idiom of this story, which, though I call it story, bears every mark of historic fact, is a Jewish scriptural idiom, and the tradition which quickens it runs back through the history of the Jews at least as far as Abraham. The heart of the tradition is the ideal of the theocratic nation set in the context of a pastoral social economy. That is exactly the note of this idyll. It paints a scene which every devout Jew dreams of secretly in his heart. It is the picture of a small faithful remnant of simple, kind, pious people, whose prayers and worship are so constant that these spiritual values seep into and colour all they do. As you read, you see what the Jewish scriptures, through all their many aberrations, were always aiming at. The ideal nation of God must be a people nourishing their souls by expectant, patient waiting upon him, while they feed themselves from the 'milk and honey' of their own land, and the old people gossip peacefully and the children play securely in the streets.

Now the little circle of inter-related people in Nazareth, the holy family, are this old dream at last come true, but painfully diminished in scale. What Isaiah had prayed for on a national scale, had come true at last, but only for perhaps a score of people. Upon this circle God broke into our human history through the faithful obedience to himself of a Jewish girl at her prayers, who had been taught to pray and taught to believe by her membership in this little circle of pastoral piety. They were politically quite insignificant and uninfluential, but they were the last fruit and the best of the many centuries of God's redemptive plan. They were the small speck of pure gold at the bottom of the prospector's pan. All else in that pan was dross and had been thrown away. The single shining speck was all that was left to show for centuries of struggle and hope and failure.

The first thing that will strike everybody who will one day read this story is that these simple, blessed people were expectant and in a special and creative way. They seem intuitively to have realised that the redemption of Israel was to rest upon them, and their obedience to the order of God. But this was a faith, not an opinion. People such as they did not make a careful analysis of the political probabilities. They took what came to them in the air they breathed and the scriptures they studied, and this was the imminent intervention of God. Both Gentiles and Jews were dreaming of a divine Saviour, and such dreams are spread by the winds, more than by books. But they had their scriptures to define and verify the dreams, and from these scriptures they drew the certainty that this divine deliverance would come upon and through the Jews, that the shape of it would be a human person, giving for tokens the signs of a human helplessness, and that in some mysterious and incredible way they themselves would have a crucial part to play in the process. The faith was in their keeping. They waited expectantly for God to act, and when he did, they obeyed him.

The tremendous appeal of the story seems to me to rest on the conjunction of pastoral simplicity with overwhelming destiny on a scale of cosmic importance. Never were the strings of human fate held in hands so simple and unassuming.

They simply waited, and continued meanwhile with the great trivialities of their ordinary lives. But when the fullness of the time was come, to use a phrase you and Paul are fond of, strange and seemingly frightening things began to happen. Angels appeared from nowhere, without any warning, and conversed familiarly with them. Stars moved out of their courses. The ordinary natural process of birth was set aside. But they seemed neither afraid, nor particularly surprised, but matched the angels themselves in the matter-of-factness with which they took what came. It was all, one would think, so uncanny, so alarming. But it did not seem so to them; and there is no more charming and less frightening story in the world than the one written in the scroll before me.

These were people who, when moved, broke spontaneously into great poetry to express themselves. They needed no poets to sing for them. They made their songs themselves, and these songs are fit to be immortal. There are three of them in the scroll. The first is Mary's. When each was carrying her unborn child, Mary went to visit Elizabeth, and when they met they were exalted. 'Blessed art thou among women, and blessed is the fruit of thy womb. And whence is this to me that the mother of my lord should come to me', cried Elizabeth. Mary, high and lifted up, answered with this song.

> My soul doth magnify the Lord: and my spirit hath rejoiced in God my Saviour.
> For he hath regarded: the lowliness of his handmaiden.
> For behold, from henceforth: all generations shall call me blessed.
> For he that is mighty hath magnified me: and holy is his Name.
> And his mercy is on them that fear him: through all generations.
> He hath shewed strength with his arm: he hath scattered the proud in the imagination of their hearts.
> He hath put down the mighty from their seat: and hath exalted the humble and meek.
> He hath filled the hungry with good things: and the rich he hath sent empty away.

> He remembering his mercy hath holpen his servant Israel: as he promised
> to our forefathers, Abraham and his seed, for ever.

It is so lovely that it catches at the heart. But you see how revolutionary a song it is. Only by twisting language and torturing words can one 'spiritualise' verses like

> He hath scattered the proud in the imagination of their heart;
> He hath put down the mighty from their seat, and hath exalted the
> humble and meek.
> He hath filled the hungry with good things, and the rich he hath sent
> empty away.

Those are unquestionably what the men of political authority call Revolutionary Sentiments and Dangerous Thoughts. But the revolution dreamed of is novel and original. It would never enter into the heads of the cunning counsellors of the world. For this is the revolution made by God, and out of his mercy, not out of his severity.

> His mercy is upon them that fear him.
> He remembering his mercy hath holpen Israel.

Like every revolutionary dream, this one contemplates the turning upside down of the social order of the world and all its values. But the first-fruit of this social reversal, because it is made by divine mercy, takes the blessed Mary precisely in her 'lowliness' and raises her to the very pinnacle of human greatness. A revolution which exalts such as her to the place of highest degree is one which no one need fear, and is the only kind of revolution in which everybody is set free, everybody is victorious and no one is left crying, in chains, or plotting revenge. The Gospel which eventually will do all this for the whole world begins here in Mary's obedience.

Another poem in this scroll was spoken by Zacharias, the

father of John the Baptist, when his son was born. It is a very fine poem, but I am not copying it for you because, somehow, it pleases me less than the others. I think this is due to its atmosphere of Jewish exclusiveness. It is the God of Israel who is blessed, the dynasty of David in which salvation comes, and this deliverance performs the mercy promised to Israel's heroes and the oath sworn to the patriarch Abraham. Twice Zacharias says that this deliverance consists in being saved from the Jews' enemies, who are regarded as automatically filled with hatred for Israel. It is Israel whose sins are to be forgiven through the prophetic life of the child John, and those to whom the song promises that they will find light in darkness and peace while lying in the shadow of death are Jews. There is no single word which envisages the least idea that any part of the Gentile world is to be ever included in this promised joy; and this is an attitude which I am still Gentile enough to resent a little.

There is a third song, little but exquisite. When Jesus had been born Mary and her husband took him to the Temple in Jerusalem, to 'present him to the Lord' and to pay the customary dues. They found there an old man and an old woman, who 'departed not from the Temple but served God with fastings and prayer day and night'. We all know the type. The thoughtless give them cruel names like 'Typical Church Mice' because their beauty and their strength have left them, and in their long loneliness they have grown eccentric habits and odd ways. Yet on their frail and feeble shoulders they carry a world, like Atlas, by the steady faithfulness of their prayers. They had been waiting 'for the consolation of Israel', and when they saw the infant Jesus they knew that here was the promise, come true at last. So Simeon (the old man's name) took the child in his arms, and sang this song:

> Lord, now lettest thou thy servant depart in peace; according to thy word.

> For mine eyes have seen; thy salvation,
> Which thou hast prepared: before the face of all people;
> To be a light to lighten the Gentiles: and to be the glory of thy people
>   Israel.

Here, surely, is perfection. I will not spoil it for you by comment.

You see the quality of the scroll the inn-keeper gave me, and you understand that I feel almost as exalted as Mary did. I like to think that when at last all this is written in my book, and when that book passes down the ages among each generation of Christian people, those songs will be read with delight and recited for their beauty. It may be so. They need no effort to remember them for they sing themselves into the memory. Perhaps it may even come to pass one day that Mary's song and Simeon's will be sung in worship throughout the breadth of the world, for we have no hymns so incomparably lovely as these.

I feel like a man who has been trafficking with angels' music. But, having been caught up into an author's heaven of heavens, I must now return to this world, carrying this unique and incomparable treasure with me, and praying for a right judgement to treat it worthily. I am now going back to Paul at Caesarea, and will stay by his side until my next step is shown me. I think my peripatetic work in Palestine is finished. I hope for an interval of sedentary peace, for I have weeks of work ahead of me in tidying all my notes.

Theophilus to Luke   ROME
                                                      A.D. 59

I CALCULATE that there is just enough time for this letter to reach you in Caesarea before the date on which the Governor Festus has arranged for Paul's passage and yours to Rome. You see that I know much about your affairs. I have heard about your travels in Palestine, and I have full reports of the preliminary hearing of Paul's case before Felix, and of his fuller but inconclusive trial before King Agrippa. But very little of this knowledge has come from yourself, O most silent of friends. Your proper chastisement shall be postponed until I see you face to face, and can administer it in speech.

For this letter has two purposes. The first is to say that I am arranging for word to be passed to me as soon as your ship docks at Puteoli. That will be the signal for great activity in my household. The best room in it will be made ready, the choicest food procured, the water made warm for the washing of travel-stained feet, and clean new garments provided for my guest who will then come to honour me. It is too long, much too long, dear friend, since we met face to face, and I am counting on you to stay with me. To have you to myself and under my own roof for a time will be the greatest pleasure life can offer me, and I dare to think, it will not be distasteful to you. We shall have so many old threads to take up again, and perhaps more new ones to unravel. Do you realise that when last we met we were both searching for a faith to live by and despairing of ever finding one? (Yes, it is as long ago as that!) And now we have both found it and have come to rest on the same spiritual rock. Silvanus' visit a year ago removed my last doubts. When I have talked with you, I mean to ask Paul for baptism, and then take the consequences, whatever they may be. They may be serious. Our young master is most capricious. On Monday he will be a saint, on Tuesday a grave philosopher, on Wednesday a scapegrace, on Thursday a statesman, and on Friday a sportsman. There are two days left in the week. What he can be on those days is best not asked. He takes more and more colour, you see, from his family circle, and that circle is lasciviously consistent every day. Those who know him best know only this, that they deal every day with an unpredictable enigma. Lately he has shown no interest whatever in the Christians. But I have not forgotten his oblique warning of a year or more ago. Nor has he. I am ready to suffer if I must, but not before my heart has been warmed and my spirit fortified by a sight of you, and I do not intend to be in a prison when you come. Besides this, I want to reach some certainty in the things in which I have been instructed. If I am to take these risks for the Lord, I must know better him in whom I am learning to believe. I know the great doctrines—Incarnation, Atonement, Resurrection; but I do not know sufficient of the more daily facts of his life, if I may put it so, on which they rest. No one here has a tenth part of your knowledge of them, and I want you to impart that knowledge to me.

The future of Paul is my other reason for writing. You were present at his hearing before King Agrippa and you know what passed. Had he not appealed to Rome he must, under Roman law, have been set free, and his guards removed. In that case he would now be dead for the Jewish assassins would certainly have got him. But by appealing he enmeshed himself inextricably in the Roman legal machine, and I cannot get him out of it. But what I can do, and have already done, is to arrange that his custody here, though real, is not unpleasant and not inconvenient for his work. I have taken the liberty of leasing a private house for him a few hundred yards from this one. There he may live, and from there he may go quite freely about his business, subject only to the guardianship by day and night of one soldier. You may be sure that I have chosen discreet men for the sharing of this duty, whom he will find pleasant to have about him. All this you may tell him after the ship has cast off from Caesarea, but not before. It would not be helpful for either Festus or King Agrippa to know it; and therefore only Paul is to be told, and no one else.

All this is partly for Paul's sake, more for yours, most of all for mine. If it is written that I am to die, I must first eat, drink, and be merry for a space with you.

Mark to Luke ROME
A.D. 62

THOUGH we both now live in the same city, though we are both Christians, yet we seem very seldom to meet. I am closely tied to my own master, Peter, in whose company life is both exacting and exciting, while you move chiefly within the orbit of Paul and the excellent Theophilus, and the paths of these two circles do not often touch. All the old trouble between Peter and Paul, and also between Paul and myself, is long ago forgiven. But it is not forgotten, and I think it has to be accepted that our two circles, though indeed united in the Lord, do better work for him if each circle keeps to its own sphere.

But you and I are bound together by a different concern which we share. Both of us, it seems, have been moved to try to put down on paper all we can discover about the events of the Lord's life on earth, believing that unless someone does so while those who shared those blessed years with him still live, much of the precious knowledge which Christians down the ages ought to possess for the healing of their souls will be irretrievably lost. It was not until a·very short time ago that I heard that you too had been giving yourself to this work, and each of us must have been trying to do the same thing, quite independently. Nor can the trails we must have left in our separate searches for information ever have crossed, though for this there is a very good reason. Your knowledge, so I am told, has been gathered from many witnesses in Palestine. Mine has nearly all come from my master Peter himself.

How far you have got, I don't know, but I finished my book

a month or two ago, and now I have had several copies made of it. Blessed be the Emperor at least for this that he has provided for authors such an excellent and efficient system of professional copyists, whereby manuscripts can be quickly and accurately multiplied! The work proved to be very exacting. That I ever began it is due to two circumstances, and the first of these is yourself.

Do you remember that night in Antioch when, after telling the brethren in the church what I remembered of the events of the night of the Lord's betrayal in the garden, you took me home with you and cross-questioned me for hours to find out what else I knew of his life? I have never forgotten that night. It was delightful and humiliating—delightful for your courtesy and kindness to one who was at that time suffering under a cloud of his own making, and humiliating because your questioning quickly exposed to me the sad depth of my ignorance of a subject on which, just before, I had almost been posing as an expert. No, of course you never intended to humiliate me: that you would never do to any man. But I did feel humbled just the same when I realised how disgracefully little I knew of the Lord I belonged to, even though my family had almost from the beginning followed him. The Last Supper was actually held in our house. That talk quickened my imagination, and provided the impetus to set to work to remedy my ignorance. I expect that most people who have the luck to talk with you are as stimulated as I was.

The other circumstance to which this book owes its origin is the sudden wrath one day of Peter. You know perhaps that several others have taken in hand the same task as our own, and, to be frank, a sad mess some of them have made of it. They seem to think that piety demands of them that they should invent miracles of all kinds for the Lord, and that devoutness relieves them of any obligation to be bound by the actual truth of what happened. The Lord's miracles, as you and I both know, formed only one part of his ministry, and invariably he had a clear and obvious reason for doing them. In fact, it is true to say that the Lord resorted to the use of his own special and overriding powers only when there was no other way to do what plainly needed to be done. In miracles, as in all else, he always showed a wonderful economy in his use of the resources he had. But too many of these writers, not content with inventing miracles which certainly never took place, draw a picture of the Lord as a miracle worker and nothing more. And the miracles they father upon him are often so silly and pointless. They show him, for example, playing in a clay pit as a little boy, and making clay birds, which no doubt he may well have done, and then these clay birds suddenly come to life, spread their wings and fly away. Very pretty no doubt, but also very silly, and even very immoral since it is a flouting of truth.

Such a book came to Peter one day when I was with him, and he read it with a running commentary of anger. 'This sort of lying simply will not do', he said, 'this is not the Lord I knew, but a stranger whom none of us would have dreamed of serving. This man makes him the hero of a fairy story!' So he ordered me to write down the truth as he remembered it, and he would help me.

So it was that I began. This book of the Lord's life which I now send you rests chiefly on Peter's own memory. He did not dictate it to me. I took notes of his teaching about it in the churches we visited, and then I put them together in a consecutive narrative. But the word 'consecutive' does not mean that I think that I have got all the events in their actual historic order. I know I have not, but also that no one can. Too much time has now passed for that kind of historic accuracy to be any longer possible. I am quite sure that you too have found or will find that this is so.

I send the book to you as an absolutely free gift. That is to say, I make no claim whatsoever to any 'rights' in it. Those who engage themselves in a task so important and indeed so holy can have no exclusive rights to claim. The vital thing is to find and proclaim the truth, and that can only be done by the co-operation of competent writers. Any spirit of competition must destroy the true purpose we all serve. So I send it now to you for you to use exactly as you wish. If there are things in it which you do not already know, use them freely. Anything which seems to you wrong or unworthy in the telling, correct. This is my book which soon is to be given to the church. But it is also yours as a gift and a thank-offering. May the Lord bless both of us in our work for him, and guide the pens of any who follow us.

Luke to Mark

ROME
A.D. 62

I HAVE received many gifts in my life, but of them all only one other has ever brought me such joy and pleasure as yours. When I lived in Greece I knew many writers and most of them were delightful people, frank and open in their speech and generous in their lives. But towards their own writings they were niggard misers. They guarded them jealously from the sight of all men, and could seldom bear that anyone should even ask them questions about them. To ask any of them, 'Are you writing anything now?' or 'What are you going to write next?' was to produce in almost all those Greek writers an embarrassed and even resentful silence. It is a curious fact, and it seems to be almost a characteristic of authorship. I have sometimes caught myself displaying the same instinct.

But there is one author of whom none of this is true, and his name is John Mark. How could you bear to let so great a book as this out of your hands? For great it certainly is. And, still more remarkable, how did you bring yourself to allow another writer to incorporate your masterpiece into his writings on the same theme, and almost invite him to change and to mangle your golden sentences according to his desire? Yours is a wonderful generosity, and I can never thank you enough for it. But the explanation is plain. We both serve the same Lord, and are both called to serve him most of all with our pens, so that between us it is impossible that there should be anything other than the glad and free co-operation of colleagues.

I need not tell you that I have read your book with all the fascinated absorption of a brother specialist, and it deepened very considerably my own gathered knowledge of the Lord.

I hope, too, that it deepened my devotion to him and en-
riched my prayers and worship, but of that I will not write
now. I am thinking now only of the problems which arise for
anyone who is trying to write of the Lord's life and work on
earth. You know even better than I what they are, and your
book has solved at least some of them for me. In particular,
your book does much to fill up several obvious and glaring
gaps in the plan of my narrative. I should tell you, by the way,
that I have not yet begun to write my own: I have a great many
notes, and I am trying now to produce a preliminary draft
of the course of the narrative; but at present that is all. It looks
as though my own book will be much fuller than yours at the
beginning and at the end, for I have found out much which
hardly anyone else knows about the infancy of the Lord, and
I have collected a wealth of resurrection stories which, as it
seems, you haven't heard. But my narrative, from the tempta-
tion of the Lord by Satan in the wilderness (which you omit,
though this must be for some purpose of your own since Peter
must plainly have heard of it) down to the triumphal entry of
the Lord into Jerusalem five days before he was crucified,
looked like being thin and meagre until your book came. It
fills in many gaps and it answers many questions. Be sure that
I shall use it to the full, and always with a special prayer for the
blessing of its author.

It would be tedious for both of us if I were to comment ex-
haustively on the details of your book, so many of them fresh
to me. So I content myself with making two more general
comments, and then by indicating the kind of use I hope to
make of your fine book in my own when eventually I come to
the actual writing of it.

First, then, when I put side by side in my mind the total of
what you and I have separately discovered, the sum of our
knowledge makes a credible and consistent picture of the
Lord. Such a one as these two documents describe is as a mere

matter of fact unique in history, and what the church claims for him is, on this evidence, not incredible and not fantastic. That is to say that between us we cannot have wholly failed in a task almost as difficult as it is important. But I am uneasily conscious, as I expect you are, of a weakness in our portrait, or, if you like, a gap in the outline drawing. We present between us a sufficiency of healing miracles to make it plain that the Lord gave no small part of his time to healing the sick. We have made it clear that he did much of his teaching by the use of parables. We show how he trained his disciples, and how and why he fell foul of the Pharisees. But we do not at present show people what his teaching was about the way Christians should behave, and what their moral values ought to be. I know that he was not merely a teacher of ethics, but he did teach ethics among other things. But of this side of his teaching, apart from parables, we seem at present to have all too few examples. I shall not be content until I find out more about this. I have vaguely heard—I wonder if you have heard it too—that someone (I don't know who) has compiled in writing a book of some of the moral addresses or sermons he gave from time to time. So far I have not succeeded in getting on the track of this book, and if you know where a copy is to be had I should be grateful beyond words if you could tell me.

The second general comment I make with a good deal of diffidence. It is, if I may say so, that your narrative strikes me as a little out of balance. I am a Greek, you see, and I cannot shake off my ingrained Attic critical habits. Call it academic if you like, but the fact is that the Greek does like his narrative to have shape and order, and also a due balance of emphasis between its different parts. Now yours seems to me to start very abruptly, with hardly any preparation of the reader for what is to come. But the really serious fault of balance seems to me to lie in the fact that you give a whole third of your space to the events of a single week out of a ministry of three years. And even of that week you describe only the first five days. You have hardly any resurrection narrative, and you content yourself with simply stating that it happened. The practical result of this fault of balance is that your story of the Passion of the Lord gives the impression of an event utterly grim, black, and hopeless, and offers to the readers no single syllable of comfort anywhere. Of course, it is true that you are describing the most horrible crime which ever happened or could ever happen—grim indeed and black indeed, but not surely hopeless. No, not even if the entire story had ended with the Lord's burial. There was real hope to be won for men and women from the very bearing of the prisoner under his cruel afflictions. I am sure you do not really doubt this, but to concentrate almost your whole emphasis on the betrayal and crucifixion of the Lord does tend to extract from the story much of the hope which lies so plainly at the heart of it when we read it as a whole with each part in due balance with every other part. The Gospel we preach is not the Cross and the Resurrection only, but is the Good News arising out of the whole of the life of the Son of God among us.

In passing, I have one other comment on your Passion narrative. When Jesus hung on the Cross you quote only one thing he said, and that the cry of despair, 'My God, my God, why hast thou forsaken me?' But he uttered other cries than this. He prayed aloud for the forgiveness of the soldiers who nailed him to the Cross. He forgave one of the thieves crucified alongside him because he asked it, and promised that 'this day shalt thou be with me in paradise'. And at the end he died in serene, quiet composure. He passed to God with the words on his lips which every Jewish child is taught to use in his prayers every night, 'Into thy hands I commend my spirit'. There was peace and calm at his ending. Some of all this I discovered from eyewitnesses of the scene while I was in Palestine, particularly from a Roman soldier I came across in Caesarea who was one of the squad detailed to perform the execution of Jesus and to guard him till he died. From first to last, you see, this man was present and heard and saw all that passed. The experience broke and changed him. For private and personal reasons this soldier had been in a state of cynical despair, but what he witnessed on that day drove out the despair and gave him back his hope. He has not become a Christian because he cannot bring himself to believe that the resurrection of the Lord is true. But from the bearing of the prisoner on the Cross, and from that alone, he found that the springs of his life were renewed. Black crime as it was, this man proved in his own experience that there is a principle of hope unquenchable at the centre of it. That principle would still be there even if, on the third day, the tomb had not been found empty.

You will naturally want to know how I think of using the book of which you so generously make me free. I have not yet begun to write the final draft of mine, and it may be some little time before I do, perhaps as much as two or three years. Apart from any other reason for this delay, it must be as clear to Peter and yourself as it is to me here that a great storm is gathering strength to break in all its fury on the Christians of Rome, and that the centre of the storm will be wherever Paul is. To him I am bound by every tie of friendship, devotion, and gratitude, and he is coming to rely more and more on my presence. My first duty is to stand by his side and to see him through whatever may be ahead, and only when that has been thoroughly done can I retire into my own 'desert place by myself' to do this work of writing to which God has called me. Nevertheless, I am taking the precaution almost at once of taking all my notes and your book to a safe place, known to no one but myself and one other.

When the time comes, then, I shall incorporate great blocks of your material, in fact practically the whole of it, into my own narrative. But I shall feel quite free to re-arrange the order of your episodes as may suit my purpose, to expand some of them as fresh material comes my way, and to contract others. But I am going to venture something else which may cause you to raise your eyebrows, and this is to soften some of your frankness of speech when you describe the failures and blindnesses of the apostles. You have drawn almost everything you have written from the apostle Peter, and he in his wonderful humility always underlines with thick black strokes in all his teaching those scenes in the Lord's life where he failed him. I have heard him many times myself, and I know how black he paints himself. But except for the denial of Jesus in the Passion, Peter was practically always in the company of some or all of the other apostles on the occasions when he failed in understanding, endurance, or courage. He thus gives the unintentional impression that all his friends shared all his faults, and this may not always be true and sometimes was not true. I feel bound, therefore, to guard against the danger of even suggesting that when Peter was obtuse all the rest were obtuse with him, when Peter failed they all failed too. I know very well that in their different ways almost all these apostles failed the Lord, and sometimes all together in the same way. But it was not true of Peter or of any of them that their 'failures' were unattended by 'successes', and on any fair balance their 'successes' loom larger in the story.

Of course, it is true that they did very often fail him. Which of us does not? And this truth must be clearly written rather than concealed by any historian worthy of the name. But it is not the whole truth about them. One part of this truth is what they have since become, and we know them to be, the fearless and inspired rulers of the churches, strong in their unimpeachable integrity, in whose strength our weaknesses are fortified and made strong. There is not one of us who does not know this to be true, and anyone who is called to write of them in the short years of their apprenticeship and training must do it in such a way as to make their early weakness not inconsistent with their later strength. It is the invincibly strong Peter whom we all know now. We cannot cloak the weaknesses of the earlier Peter—he would be furious if we did—but at the same time we ought not to paint them too black.

One other thought your book has raised in my mind. But as I write I am feeling my way and am not yet sure of my mind about it. I take it that the ultimate purpose of the work you and I have been called to do is to paint in words a picture of the Lord in order that all his people may know him in whom they have believed. Now he came, and said that he came into the world to be a portrait of God his father, and also a portrait of man, the child of God. He was and is both God and man, divine and human. Therefore, any true portrait of him must do justice, and equal justice to both of these facts about him. He is our Lord and he is our brother, not one or the other but both and equally—son of man and son of God. To ask us weak and fallible authors to paint in our words a portrait of him which keeps in absolute, just balance these two contrasted sides of his nature is probably to ask more than we are capable of doing, no matter how inspired we may be. So I take it that both of us, and all who may follow us, are bound, no matter how we struggle to guard against it, to emphasise one portrait a little to the expense of the other. Now your portrait of Jesus is most certainly that of a human being. So it ought to be, and so, I hope, mine will be. It is also of course the portrait of divinity. But you do seem to me to give the humanity a very slightly greater emphasis than the divinity. Again let me emphasise that this is not fault-finding. Far from that, it is almost necessary at this moment. Most of the teaching we hear about him today does lay more stress on Jesus our Lord than on Jesus our brother. For this very reason it is time to give the very slightest of tilts to the balance. Therefore, when I come to write I intend to draw a portrait which, while true to historic fact in every detail, leaves the reader in no doubt that the hero of the story is the very Majesty of the universe.

God bless you, my brother. You have made me a very, very grateful man. Some day I intend to pay a small part of my debt to you by sending you a copy of my own book, and I hope you may be alive to read it. But the church in Rome is presently going to provide the Lord with many martyrs. That is obvious. I can only hope that John Mark will not be one of them, but that his calling will be to stay for a time in the world with those whom the Lord leaves here to be his witnesses.

Luke to Silvanus   SYRACUSE
                                                        A.D. 64

IN far distant Bithynia you will not yet have heard our sad,
lamentable news, and it falls to my lot to tell it to you. I
will not cloak it with gentle prefaces, but will tell you at once
that Paul, our dear master and friend, is dead, executed in a fit
of rage by that bloodthirsty young ruffian Nero. Theophilus,
most excellent and tried friend of us both, is banished to his
villa in the Island of Capri; and I am likewise exiled to Achaia,
and am waiting here for a boat to take me through the Ionian
Sea. For both of us the sentence is life if we stay in our places of
exile and death if we ever leave them. So I suppose Theophilus
and I will never again meet in this world. Our old partnership
of Philippian days is irretrievably broken now. And all this is
but a herald of the real storm that is gathering strength to burst
upon the church in Rome. Christian blood is soon to flow in
torrents, but only to be the seed of the greater church to
come. Theophilus prophesied it, and that cool and far-sighted
old statesman was right.

But I must tell you the whole story from the beginning. You
spent some time with Theophilus before Paul and I came to
Rome two years ago so you already know of the Emperor's
early suspicion of the church, and of the hint he gave Theophilus that it might be dangerous for him to have too much
to do with Christians. That was still the position when we
came to Rome, and for quite eighteen months there was no
hint of imperial disapproval. Theophilus continued with his
instruction for baptism by Paul and myself. Paul had consider-
able freedom of movement, subject only to the presence of
one guard. He visited all the churches in Rome and many of

those in other Latin cities. He spent many many hours writing letters to the churches in Philippi, Thessalonica, and elsewhere and to personal friends and disciples of his own choosing, like Timothy and Titus. I plied my trade as a physician, and I think I owe to that the fact that I am still alive, for I was soon attending on many of Caesar's household, and two of his special favourites I brought back to health when they were nearly dead of the plague. I wish their lives showed signs of being more worth the saving but of course a doctor cannot think of that. At least they seem to have had a spark of the grace of gratitude, so there may yet be some hope for them. I think myself we were all doomed from the moment that Theophilus put himself under Paul's instruction, but that the sentence was deferred for the time because Theophilus with his long experience of imperial affairs of state was indispensable to the Emperor until he had had time to pass on his knowledge.

The calm was broken when the Empress Poppaea, an infamous woman if ever there was one, was persuaded by her Jewish relations, some of whom had been Paul's sworn enemies for years, to beguile Nero to move against him. So, you see, the Jews in the end had their revenges, though I think it would all have happened just the same if Procula rather than Poppaea had been sitting by the Emperor's side. The Emperor moved very gradually. He increased Paul's restrictions, doubled his guards, and suborned his servants. It was at that time that his personal servant Demas fled for his life. Paul naturally knew what was happening and saw ahead of him the inevitable end of it all. So he sent away as many of his followers as he could. Cresceus was sent to Galatia and Titus to Dalmatia to look after the churches there, and he saved John Mark's life by arranging with Peter to send him to join forces with Titus later on in Ephesus. All this left Paul alone in his house, so I left Theophilus to go to look after him, and I stayed with him to the very end.

Then Theophilus came. The time had come, he said, for him to declare himself openly as a committed Christian. He had measured the price and was ready to pay it. He therefore asked for baptism, but from hands other than Paul's. 'And why not at my hands?' asked Paul. 'Because if you baptise me you are like to sign your death warrant thereby'. But it was no good arguing. Paul resolutely insisted that his hands and none other should pour the water, his finger and none other should trace on his forehead the sign of the Cross. He knew then, I think, that his course was really run. So he had his way. With the church around him he baptised Theophilus, and laid his hands on him, and they all escorted him triumphantly to the place of the Eucharist, and administered to him for the first time the blessed bread and wine.

It was for the last time too, for after that events marched swiftly. None of us ever saw Theophilus again. He was arrested that night, and next morning was on his way to perpetual exile in Capri. Then it was my turn. I was bound and taken into the imperial presence. Nero wasted no time on me. 'Paul is to die at midnight. You are among those who have dared to defy me and you, master physician, deserve to die with him. Is this your wish, for since you healed my friends I will grant you one wish?' 'No, your majesty', I replied, 'I must not claim the privilege of dying with him. The God whose I am and whom I serve has other work I must do before I can depart hence and be at peace with him. My wish is that I may be with Paul until the end and share all his last hours'. 'You have your wish', said the Emperor coldly. Then he sneered. 'You Christians are not so brave after all; you flinch at the sight of an executioner's axe. But I add this, that when Paul is dead, you are to be gone from Rome at once to make your way to Achaia, and as long as your life lasts you will remain in that province. If you leave it, you die'. I bowed myself out without another word. I own to you that the taunt of cowardice stung, but both you and Paul know why I may not yet be martyred.

The rest is quickly told. Paul had been removed to the prison and the guards took me to him there. He was in a cell, and two guards with him. They were decent kindly men who had grown to love Paul, and hated what they had to do. They placed no restrictions on us, bade us talk as freely as if they were not there, promised to forget all we said, and when the time drew near procured for us the bread and wine for our last Communion together.

How shall I tell you of those last few hours of talk together? It was too intimate, too sacred to be written. You must come some day to see me, and then I will tell you all, for every word spoken in those hours is carved imperishably in my mind. You would expect Paul to be cheerful, and at times even jocular, and so he was. He it was who set himself to comfort me, and his guards too. What strength we had was his strength. He needed none from us, and indeed we had little to give. I think he was glad to go. 'I have finished my course: I have kept the faith', he said many times, 'and now I go to God. All that keeps me from the last and best of all journeys is one short, sharp flash of pain. Why should I fear that? You and I, old friend, have known worse many times'. He spoke a good deal of the work still remaining for me to do, and he drifted for a time into a reverie of prayer, as the Lord did after supper on the night of his arrest, and the words and phrases of his prayer he drew from many sentences he had written in letters to his churches. But all the time I kept glancing at the hourglass on the table, and watching the grains of sand drop inexorably one by one. The falling of the last, the guards told us, was the moment of doom.

When the time was nearly done, they brought bread and wine, and Paul did the Eucharist for us both. Of that most sacred moment I cannot write. Then a spear haft hammered on the door, and when it was opened, a squad of soldiers entered, the executioner with his axe leading them. 'Paul, it is time to be brave', he said according to the formula. 'And why should I not be brave', said Paul, 'You do but send me to the haven where I would be.' I made to go with him, but a guard touched my arm and said, 'No, you are to stay here till it is all over.' So with a gesture of benediction and a smile he went out with the soldiers, and I recited for him the *Proficiscere Anima* for those on the point of death.

> Go forth on thy journey from this world, O Christian Soul.

But there was no time to finish the commendations, for as I was reciting it the footsteps went Tramp! Tramp! Left! Right! and I could just hear Paul calling out, as Stephen had called before him, 'Lord Jesus, receive my spirit.' And then there was silence, and a momentary shuffling, and then one slow, heavy thud. 'May thy portion this day be in peace, and thy dwelling in the heavenly Jerusalem.'

So there passed to his great reward and to his true home the greatest, the most lovable, the most original man I have ever known, my spiritual father, my companion, at times my patient, and always my friend. By any standard he was the greatest among us all, and his achievement was beyond our measuring. For hundreds upon hundreds of years, I believe, Christian people of all colours and all lands even to the scorched and frozen corners of the world will be warming their souls at the fires he has lit. And you and I have had the luck to be his intimate and daily friends. For such as him one does not mourn. One goes on one's way rejoicing and with hope. My way now leads to Megara. I am ready to write, and I know where to look for a house. Write to me there, and come and see me as soon as you can.

LETTER THIRTY-FOUR

Luke to Theophilus   MEGARA
A.D. 65

WHEN I was a young medical student only a few miles from here, and for the first time I was allowed to travel by myself, my dear parents made a rule that I must write to them immediately I had arrived at the end of every journey to tell them I really had arrived and was well and happy. Ever since then I have had the steady habit of announcing my arrivals to my friends.

So my first letter from my new and my last home shall be to you. I have found a house twenty miles from Athens. It is perched up on a hill above the shore, and as I sit at a table in the window of the front room I look out at the deep turquoise of the Aegean Sea, and watch the little fishing boats sail to and fro. So I in my exile watch the sea and its traffic, which I always did love; and you in yours, according to what I have heard, potter about your farm tending the roses, gathering the strawberries, and talking learnedly about the milk yield of cows and the weight of fleeces. It could be worse for us, my friend. Capri and Megara are pleasanter than Rome and Jerusalem, and though my heart aches when I think of how deep a bath of blood one city now is and the other soon will be, I cannot honestly say that I yearn ever to see either of them again. There is, too, a tiny church here for my worship, and a few patients for my physician's craft, and my work to do, and Paul's memory to hold me to it. The only other thing I could ask for is a sight of you; but then if we cannot meet again in this life, there is nothing to stop our correspondence, and no one could prevent us from praying for each other. Think of me, then, as a contented man, and tell me that you are the same.

My task awaits me. It is actually on the table in front of me, but like all writers I've ever known, I find a curious disinclination to cease from the pleasant dreaming of dreams about it, and actually to come to grips with it, pen determinedly in hand. So I write instead to you, a little aimlessly as you perceive. But there inexorably wait the four documents I must weave into a narrative—the book of Mark, who has trodden this way before me, my own large collection of notes, the Judean story of the Lord's birth, and the anonymous anthology of the Lord's ethical teaching. They speak to me peremptorily. They will wait no longer. So I begin—but how? I think with a dedication, and plainly to you, dear Excellency, who first pointed this path to me. 'To his Excellency Theophilus, that he may know the certainty of these things wherein he has been instructed'. Does that please you? I have just written it down, the very first words on a virgin scroll. So I have begun. God grant I may live to write the last words too, and that you may live to read the book when I send it to you. And so to work. God bless and keep you.